"I'm Not Afraid Of Anything, Mac," Jennifer Said Firmly.

"Now, if you would go, please, I have a lot to do."

"I'm going, but only for now."

Jennifer didn't respond. Clinging to an outward calm, she sat as she was as he strode to the door. When he stopped, his eyes meeting hers, she didn't look away.

"Make no mistake about it, Jennifer, there's unfinished business between us, and I'll be back to resolve it."

"There's nothing to resolve. After you left, my life was havoc and disorder. Peace was a long time coming, but I have it now, and I don't want to lose it." Her hand shook. "What do you really want, Mac? Why are you really here?"

Dear Reader,

Another year is drawing to a close here at Silhouette Desire, and I think it's a wonderful time for me to thank all of you—the readers—for your loyalty to Silhouette Desire throughout the years. Many of you write letters, letters that we try to answer, telling us all about how much you like the Desire books. Believe me, I appreciate all of the kind words, because let's be honest . . . without *you,* there wouldn't be any *us!*

In the upcoming year we have many sexy, exciting stories planned for you. *Man of the Month* is continuing with books by authors such as Diana Palmer, Joan Hohl, Ann Major and Dixie Browning. Ann Major's SOMETHING WILD series is continuing, as is Joan Hohl's BIG BAD WOLFE series. We will have special "months of men," and also duets from authors such as Raye Morgan and Suzanne Simms. And that's just part of the Desire plan for '94!

This month, look for a wonderful *Man of the Month* title from BJ James. It's called *Another Time, Another Place,* and it's a continuation of her stories about the McLachlan brothers. Don't miss it!

So once again, thank you, each and every one of you, the readers, for making Silhouette Desire the great success that it is.

Happy holidays from

Lucia Macro
Senior Editor . . . and the rest of us at Silhouette Desire!

BJ JAMES
ANOTHER TIME, ANOTHER PLACE

SILHOUETTE *Desire*®
™ Published by Silhouette Books
America's Publisher of Contemporary Romance

SILHOUETTE BOOKS

ISBN 0-373-05823-3

ANOTHER TIME, ANOTHER PLACE

Copyright © 1993 by BJ James

Books by BJ James

Silhouette Desire

The Sound of Goodbye #332
Twice in a Lifetime #396
Shiloh's Promise #529
Winter Morning #595
Slade's Woman #672
A Step Away #692
Tears of the Rose #709
The Man with the Midnight Eyes #751
Pride and Promises #789
Another Time, Another Place #823

BJ JAMES

married her high school sweetheart straight out of college and soon found that books were delightful companions during her lonely nights as a doctor's wife. But she never dreamed she'd be more than a reader, never expected to be one of the blessed, letting her imagination soar, weaving magic of her own.

BJ has twice been honored by the Georgia Romance Writers with their prestigious Maggie Award for Best Short Contemporary Romance. She has also received the *Romantic Times* Critic's Choice Award.

Prologue

Wine shimmered in frosted crystal. A solitary repast lay undisturbed on creamy damask. Beyond a screen of cloistering foliage a violin cried, its plaintive song rising to a canopy of glass, and a midnight sky radiant with stars.

Madame Zara's, more garden than restaurant. More ambience than reality. A mood. A thought. A memory among so many for a man who had come home.

Pushing back his chair he stood. A man older, stronger, drawn in bolder strokes by time. Shoulders that had been broad were broader now beneath a faultless jacket. A lean waist leaner in tailored trousers. His dark brown hair was streaked by an equatorial sun, his skin weathered. In wavering shadow his eyes caught the light of a candle and glittered with a dark blue flame.

With one finger he stroked an untouched glass. Frost gathered like a tear on his fingertip, and the hardness in him eased. He was, for the blink of an eye, the young man he'd been.

His hand curled into a fist. The tear that was not a tear dried against his palm. With a raggedly drawn breath and a shake of his head he turned from the table, from the night sky, and the youthfulness was gone.

Looking neither right nor left, he wound his way to the counter where Madame Zara waited. Silently, her hair a coronet of silver, the monarch of the garden watched him through the all-seeing eyes of an oracle. As he offered a sheaf of money, her hand closed over his.

He frowned and she smiled, saying, "Not tonight." Her grip tightened. "It's good to have you back, bonny Gemini."

Gemini, the name she'd given him long ago. "You remember."

"One could hardly forget you. Any of you." Then thoughtfully, with a different allusion, "Either of you."

"It's been a while. A lot has changed."

"Yes." Her bright gaze met his. "But it isn't too late."

"It was too late a long time ago," he refuted gently.

"It's never too late." She leaned nearer, and eyes a paler shade of blue bored into his. "She grieves, but love can soothe the grief that time cannot."

"The only love was mine, and the only grief."

"You're wrong. Very wrong."

He smiled a sad, grim smile, shaking his head much as he had at his solitary table.

"You will see." Her voice was low and strong, without a quiver of age.

"There's nothing to see." He drew her hand to his lips, brushing a kiss over knotted blue veins. Releasing her, he took a step back. With a small, resigned gesture he repeated, "Nothing, old friend."

Madame Zara watched as he left, remembering a gentle man. With an ache in her heart she mourned love lost.

One

_____

Jennifer McLachlan stared down at the report on her desk. Facts, figures, words that sealed Chrissie Hanyon's fate swam before her eyes, branding her brain with brutal truths.

She wanted to shred the ugly yellow sheets to confetti, and by destroying the words, destroy the disease that would make every day of this baby girl's life a living hell. She wanted to curse and shake her fist at the Fates that served an innocent child so unfairly. She wanted to weep. But all the curses and tears in the world couldn't help Chrissie.

"Why do I do this?" Her voice was hollow, the words brittle. There was no answer from the empty room, no solace in its soothing decor. But Jennifer McLachlan needed no answers. She knew why she spent her days counseling children and parents of children who were terminally ill. She knew for whom.

Laying the chart aside, she stood, turning away, wishing she could turn her mind away as easily. Standing at the window, she looked out at the gray day, and she was grateful. But would the news have been any worse if the sun were shining?

Chrissie Hanyon was dying. Not today. Not tomorrow. If she was very lucky, not this year, or the next, but too soon.

Lucky? Jennifer shivered. Arms crossed against a chill that came from within, she stared over the parking lot beneath her office window. How could buying a life a day, or a week, or a year at a time be called lucky? Why did it have to be Chrissie, whose case Jennifer hadn't been drawn into until this admission to the hospital? Why Chrissie, with soft blond curls, dark blue eyes, and just two years old?

Caught in her misery, Jennifer didn't notice that rain had finally begun. She didn't hear the bare trees of February clacking like geese before the storm's first winds. She didn't see cold drops spattering the glass or sliding in winding rivulets down panes. The world beyond the window was lost to her in a silver mist of rain and tears.

When she roused, she didn't know how long she'd stood before the window staring through the rain. Long enough that a change in shifts was completed and the parking lot deserted. Long enough that the rain had slackened, settling into a dreary drizzle.

"Foolish," Jennifer muttered at the waste of time. Drying her face, she moved to her desk. Yet something absorbed by the mind, rather than seen by the eye, something curious, had her returning to the window. Her gaze was drawn to the construction that would one day be the new wing of Barclay Medical Center for Children. Steel and concrete as bare as the bones of a prehistoric animal stood in stark relief against the lowering sky. But it wasn't the structure, nor its starkness, that drew her. It was the man who walked there, oblivious to the rain.

He moved easily, his booted step sure as the dusty excavation turned to a morass of Georgia clay. Crouching at a concrete piling, he scooped up a handful of soil, hefting it in his palm, reading it as if it were tea leaves and he a seer. He was wet from head to toe. His jeans clung to his thighs, his shirt to his broad shoulders. His hair, darkened by the rain, brushed wetly against his collar. Jennifer wondered if he'd lost his hard hat, then realized it was only discarded for the moment on a piling nearby. Even without the distinctive blue hat, by his manner he was clearly a member of the construction crew. Just as clearly something about the rain and soil bothered him.

His problem, not hers, and she should have dismissed him and attended to her own. Yet something kept her standing at the window watching. Something hauntingly familiar in the way he moved, in the breadth of his shoulders, the tilt of his head.

As if he knew she watched and could read her thoughts, he tilted his head again, lifting his face and his gaze to the towering steel.

Jennifer's heart thudded too hard in her chest. She reached out to steady herself. Her fingers clutched at the heavy wood frame of the window. Her lungs labored as she stared at his handsome face.

Mac! But it couldn't be. Denying the illusion, she spun away from the window, turning her back on what couldn't be. Pacing the room, arms crossed, hands clenching and unclenching over her elbows, she forced herself to think rationally. Mac would not be in this small suburban community, nor would he be crouching in the rain gathering up handfuls of clay. But if he were, it was no concern of hers. None, she asserted as she found herself drawn again to the window.

But what if . . . ?

With the heel of her fist she scrubbed at the glass, willing the deceiving rain away. The day was still gray, the air still misted with silver, the parking lot still deserted. Had she thought it would change simply because a familiar stranger walked through the rain? Ridiculous, she decided and, steeling herself against the race of her heart and the panic of her thoughts, let her gaze move over the skeletal structure.

Rain channeled down vertical columns and dripped from intersecting girders. Puddles collected in the clay. But no man walked there with a booted step. No one knelt on the ground or lifted a rain-washed face to the sky. The site was deserted. Where had he gone so quickly? Or had she imagined more than the resemblance? Had she imagined the man?

No. She was weary, and her mind bruised by the bitter truths she must cope with daily, but she hadn't yet sunk to the escapism of total fabrication. The man was real, if not the look.

With that bit of relief she was determined to forget the foolish incident.

At her desk she picked up Chrissie's file. Chrissie, whose likeness had provoked Jennifer's descent into this fugue of delusion. Her file comprised two reports. Two tersely worded pages that solved the puzzle of unexplained fevers and swollen glands, and determined the future of a beautiful child.

Jennifer couldn't deal with those ghastly, tissue-thin pages. Not again. But there was no need. The diagnosis was engraved on her mind.

Leukemia.

Putting the hurtful papers aside, she leaned her head against the supple leather of her chair. Closing her eyes to shield them from the light, she found herself drifting. Remembering.

Remembering when a young man like the stranger in the rain had loved her....

"Well, hello!" Jennifer Burke lifted her face to the solemn young man who towered over her, and she offered her hand. She hadn't intended such formality when she'd wrangled this meeting through mutual acquaintances, but when he stood, acknowledging her with courtly, old-fashioned charm, a lesser response would have been clumsy. Jennifer Burke was a lot of things, but clumsy wasn't one of them.

"Hello, yourself, Miss Burke." His voice was low, his handclasp firm. Keeping her fingers in his, he waited as politely as before. The next move was plainly hers.

Accustomed to the more aggressive and gregarious men of her own circle, Jennifer was surprised again, and fascinated. Looking into eyes too dark to be blue, she decided to let the evening take her where it would. "My name is Jennifer."

"Robert Bruce," he responded, smiling at the name. "But friends like Rick and Karen here have declared it too much for their lazy tongues. I've been rechristened." A look at the male counterpart of the couple at his table left little doubt who was responsible. "A little redundant, I'm afraid, but it stuck, and Mac McLachlan it seems to be."

Mac McLachlan, her reason for being in this small tavern. Her reason for looking her best, for dressing in understated, provocative style. The brainy hillbilly had come out of Backwoods, Some Direction Carolina, and in his years at Georgia Tech had acquired a reputation among her friends. A ladies' man without a lady. A playboy who didn't play. She'd listened and laughed as first one girl set her sights on him, and then another. None had gotten past a smile or two, or with rare luck, a couple of dates. She'd suffered through disappointment after disappointment with halfhearted sympathy, finally wondering aloud one too many times how immune mortal man could be. Even one who was "elusive as the mist and sexy as hell."

Her observation, taken as a challenge, turned into a dare. Jennifer was bored. Jennifer never refused a dare. So here she was, out of her element, facing a dark and charming stranger who looked more like Mr. October than the aloof, supercilious graduate student she'd imagined.

She let her gaze roam unabashedly over him, appraising her quarry. Her eyes went first to his dark brown hair. Thick, healthy, worn a little longer than was stylish, falling just short of his shoulders. Reflecting on all she'd heard of his intensity, his total absorption in his studies, she suspected the length would vary as he remembered or forgot it, in turn, until the nuisance factor kicked in.

"You're a native, Jennifer?"

"Native?" From under the shadow of straight brows, his unsettling gaze was truly a dark, unforgettable blue. No trick of the light ignited the diamond-bright glitter. "Yes, of course, a native. My family has lived in Atlanta forever." Drawing a breath, she rushed on. "You're from one of the Carolinas?"

"North."

"Pardon?"

"North Carolina. My family has lived there, near a town called Madison, for some time, but hardly forever."

"I suppose no one has." He was so controlled and she was babbling. The cool and trendy Jennifer Burke never babbled.

"I was teasing you, Jennifer."

His skin was dark from the sun. The contours of his cheeks and chin were strong, prominent, unblunted by time. A face saved from severity by smooth, unlined skin and a mouth as gentle as masculine, as seductive as sensual.

Lips to tempt even the most immune.

Jennifer caught her own lip between her teeth, the swift serrated ache a return to reality. The startling thought, as spellbinding as his level gaze, was silenced, if not forgotten. Appalled, ignoring the heat that flushed the slope of her full breasts and her throat, she struggled for clinical detachment as she dared consider the rest of Mac McLachlan.

There was a disquieting timidity in her boldness, if such could be, as her eyes devoured him. As a woman who thought herself impervious committed to memory the complete man.

He was not tall as much as muscular. Yet with a leanness that belied the strength coiled in arm and shoulder. There was quietness in him, self-possession without arrogance. He was who he was, what he was, with no need to make a statement. The confidence was unassuming. As much a part of the man as his name, or the way he moved, the tone of his speech. The color of his eyes.

Clothing makes the man? In this case the reverse was true, and again he was a contradiction. The same as the men about him, but on a closer look, with that unassuming difference. He wore the casual dress of a thousand others. Sneakers, jeans, nondescript shirt of a certain price, a certain label, de rigueur for undergraduate and graduate student alike. Except his jeans, soft with age, clinging to thigh and hip, were a working man's jeans, intended for practical wear, with not a designer label in sight. His soft knit shirt, generic, lacking the definitive little logo in current fashion, fit closely over his wide shoulders and deep chest, then bloused as it was tucked about his slender waist. A combination of faded indigo and darkest burgundy, handsome, unique, only because he wore them.

Rumor had it that before his days at Tech and summers between semesters, he worked as a lumberjack in the foothills and mountains of the Carolinas. Faced with his physical size, the strength, the hard steady look of him, what she'd dismissed as lore surrounding this unlikely gallant, now she believed.

He was as powerfully and guilelessly attractive as any man she'd ever encountered.

"Mac." A no-nonsense name for a man of the same sort. A man beyond petty concerns, who had no more time to squander on being a maverick than on conforming. "The name suits you." Then, because she was standing in a smoke-filled bar with music blaring, because she felt no inclination to take her hand from his, she said again, softly, "It suits you very well."

"Are you going to stand all night holding hands, conversing like genteel strangers, or are you going to join us?"

Mac hardly looked away from her as his laughing friend tugged at his shirt. His only response was a glimmer of a smile, yet it changed his face dramatically. With a subtle shift his chiseled features were softer, and mischief sparkled in his eyes. When Jennifer had begun to think he would never answer, he spoke, and incredibly for one so thoroughly American, the clipped answer held a hint of Scotland. "No, Rick."

"Would that be, 'No, Rick, we're not going to stand here holding hands'? Or 'No, Rick, we're not going to join you'?" Rick asked from his place at the table.

Mac's smile faded, his grip on her hand tightened. "Yes."

"Yes?" The word came in unison from Rick and Karen, a serious couple for months.

"Ask an ambiguous question, expect an ambiguous answer." Mac's tone matched the bantering mood of his companions, but there was nothing ambiguous in the look in his eyes. "We'll leave it for Jennifer to interpret."

Jennifer was mute, silenced by his intense gaze. No clever, provocative comment came to mind. Whatever she expected of the night, it wasn't this sudden and riveting attraction. She'd come to engage and conquer, expecting that before many such nights were done, she would walk away with Mac McLachlan's proverbial but coveted scalp hanging from her belt.

This was a game, as her classes were games, and her social conquests. A perfect grade-point average and a string of would-be suitors were only eventualities to be shrugged aside. Tonight everything had changed. Suddenly, with a smile and the touch of his hand, she didn't understand the rules of the game.

"I'm not very good at interpretations," she managed at last. "I'll leave them to you."

Keeping her gaze, Mac nodded, his breath rising in his chest. "Yes." Overriding good-natured catcalls accusing ambiguous ambiguity, he continued, "Yes, we aren't going to stand here all night holding hands, and yes, we aren't going to join you." With a wave for Rick and Karen, he leaned closer to Jennifer. "There's a table for two in the corner. Would you join me?"

Jennifer followed his lead with no idea where it was going. "A table for two would be perfect."

"I was sure it would be," Mac commented cryptically, then released her hand only to curl his own around her shoulder to guide her through the raucous crowd. The bumping and shoving was unintentional, a by-product of overenthusiastic dancing or innocent high spirits, but an elbow, eye level for a woman as small as Jennifer, could be painful. Shielding her with his body, Mac steered her through the melee, then sat across the tiny table from her. Their knees brushed as he leaned back in his chair watching her as he might a peacock among pigeons.

"So, Jennifer, what do you think?"

Startled by his abrupt question, she pushed her heavy blond hair from her face and glanced around. "It's an interesting place."

"Sulley's is not exactly your usual sort of place. Not your side of town."

"I suppose not," Jennifer admitted. "Is it always crowded?"

"I don't know—I've only been here once before. But I wasn't asking about Sulley's, I was asking about this." His gesture included both of them.

"This?" With a sinking feeling, Jennifer suspected it was too late for innocence.

"Your conquest. Was it convincing enough to win the bet?"

"You knew!"

"That you didn't just drop in tonight? That you orchestrated the evening to prove a point? I knew."

"Karen?"

"Rick. He thought I should be forearmed."

Jennifer hadn't understood the rules of the game because they hadn't been playing the same game. The elusive prey hadn't been elusive at all and had turned the tables on her. She should've been suspicious when he'd reacted so strongly to her. Particularly when his response to her was out of sync with everything she'd ever heard about him. The warning signals were there and she'd ignored them. One look from those startling blue eyes, one smile, and she'd forgotten that the cardinal rule of girl catches boy is that girl doesn't get caught, instead.

"I suppose you're angry." She traced the pattern of the checkered tablecloth. Toyed with a drop of candle wax that flowed down the wicker-covered chianti bottle serving as the table's sole decoration. Anything to keep from looking at Mac. "You have every right to be furious."

"I was at first, and a little surprised." He laughed, a low, mesmerizing note. "And more than a little flattered."

"Surprised? Flattered?"

"Sure." He shrugged heavy shoulders. "Surprised because I'm hardly the type to merit the interest. Flattered that, misguided as it is, the interest brought you here."

Listening warily, Jennifer wondered if he had no concept of how attractive he was. How challenging. "When did you decide?"

"To help you win your bet?"

"Not to be angry."

Without a beat of hesitation or evasion, "The moment I saw you."

Jennifer looked up from the table, her hand still, her own surprise on her face.

"I'm a pushover for brown-eyed blondes."

"Blondes?" Her emphasis was on the plural.

"Blonde." Mac grinned, linking his fingers through hers. "Only so big." He measured a distance from the floor with his free hand. "And only so long as her name is Jennifer."

Tensions threading through the conversation vanished. Reasons behind their encounter became unimportant. With glances meeting and hands entwined they were laughing. Jennifer's laughter rising like a bell on a clear morning. Mac's rich, deep, as steady as the man he was.

Jennifer had fallen in love with him that night. On the heels of a silly schoolgirl prank, to the sound of their concerted laughter, she loved him as she'd never loved anyone before. Or ever again.

Everything should have been perfect, but perfect was only for fairy tales....

"Who the...?" Dressed in pajama trousers, with sleep heavy in his eyes, Mac flung open the door of his small apartment. Falling silent in mid-harangue, his expression ran the gamut from anger to surprise and back to anger. "Jennifer! What the devil are you doing here? It's four in the morning."

Stepping over the threshold, she produced a bottle of champagne, offering it to him like an olive branch. "I know what time it is. Since you wouldn't come to my birthday celebration, I brought the celebration to you."

Mac's gaze shifted to the hallway, expecting the unexpected as he always did with Jennifer.

"Don't bother looking for the rest of the party. I sent them home hours ago. This one is private."

"Are you drunk, or have you lost your mind?"

"I haven't had a drop to drink. Not even to toast my own birthday, and my mind is still very much with me."

"Then why are you really here?"

"Because I miss you." Her grip on the champagne was hard, desperate. "Mac, I can't just let you walk out of my life."

"Dammit, Jennifer!" Clasping a hand at the nape of his neck, he closed his eyes, his expression grim. "It won't work. It took me weeks to admit it, but we have nothing in common."

"You're wrong!" Jennifer fought a surge of panic. Her breasts rose in a passionate breath, thrusting against supple fabric. Her body, bare beneath the slender column of gleaming silk, tensed with the need to make him understand no difference was great enough to keep them apart. "We have the most important thing in the world in common. I love you and you love me."

"Love isn't always enough."

The hardness she'd sensed but seldom seen was in his voice, in his face. Her searching eyes could find nothing of the boyish mischief that had startled and captivated her. Nor of the tender man she wanted for her first, her only lover. He was the immutable Scot, stubborn, grim-eyed, mature beyond his twenty-four years and not to be swayed by fair and honorable methods.

But he hadn't denied he loved her.

So be it, Jennifer decided without a qualm. She had too much to lose to falter over fairness and honor.

Deliberately she closed the door, her decision made. There was no going back. Leaning against the solid wood, she watched him as the shadowy lamplight from the bedroom fell in a pale rectangle over the carpet, capturing him in its glow. She watched as the anguish he fought to hide crept into his face.

He wanted her as much as she wanted him. He was as lonely as she was without him. And tonight loneliness would be her ally.

Taking a step closer, her body moving in deceptive languor, she felt the stirring of the wanton need that had drawn her to him tonight. Her heart racing, she took another step, and another, feeling his reluctant gaze on her, knowing that he wanted to turn away and could not.

What she saw in his eyes was in her's as well. Blue silk rippling with every step became blue flames licking at her body, brushing over breasts and thighs in a heated caress. She was trembling when she stopped. Her voice roughened with fear and passion, and the wonder of her own daring. "We come from different worlds, different backgrounds, yet those very differences drew us together."

"I should have known better."

She heard the bitterness. With himself, with her, with what they were. What they weren't. "Tell me where it's written that money should matter, or social position. Tell me when any difference is more important than love."

"Jennifer, this isn't the time or place to discuss this."

"When is the time? You've avoided me for days."

"I thought it would be easier."

"For whom?"

She was so close the scent of her perfume enveloped him. Exotic, expensive, underscoring the disparity of their lives. "For both of us." Mac sighed again, wearily. "I thought it would be easier for both of us."

She had startled him from deep sleep, but his haggard face told her it was sleep that was as rare for him as for her. "You were wrong." Her fingertips brushed over his face, tracing the lines that bracketed his mouth.

"Jennifer." His voice was a forbidding rasp, but he didn't draw away.

"Tell me you don't love me," she said softly, ignoring the harshness she heard. "Say you don't want me and I'll go."

"This is madness." A hand raked through his hair, bringing no order to it. He'd forgotten to have it trimmed, or hadn't bothered, and it tumbled down his neck in a wild disheveled mane.

"It's only madness if you don't love me." Rising on tiptoe, she stroked his hair into order. Her touch was tender. When he accepted her caress in silence, she grew surer. It was the most natural of acts to curl her body into his. Not even a stubborn Scot's decree that it was wrong could vanquish desire. Jennifer nestled against him, her breasts beneath their whimsical veil of silk crushed against his bare chest. She heard his gasp catch in his throat, felt him tremble as she was trembling, yet he didn't recoil from her. "Say you don't love me and I'll walk through that door and if we're careful our paths will never cross again."

He turned his head away, shielding his face from her.

"Say it." Tangling her hand in his hair she drew his head down to hers, her lips teased over his. "Say this isn't real. Tell me your body lies, that you don't want to make love to me. That it isn't more important than any difference between us."

He grasped her waist in a hard, cruel grip. A muscle rippled in his cheek. There was anger in him, and the darkness of an endless night. It was a stranger's hot, tormented eyes that stared down at her. A stranger's stern face she stroked. Jennifer stood her ground, waiting, hoping.

His eyes closed, shuttering his burning gaze from her. His head turned into her palm. His lips were a brand against her flesh. "Jennifer."

Her name, a painful, guttural cry for reason that was lost. As he drew her to him at last, the champagne she'd offered fell forgotten to the carpet.

Champagne at dawn. A strong, proud man who loved her and wanted her forever. At twenty, Jennifer believed her world was complete. With Mac's arms around her, his cheek resting against her hair, she toasted the rising run. Lifting her face to its bright new radiance, she never dreamed that before the year was done, pride would tear her world asunder, and not even love would survive....

"For the last time, no, Jennifer." Stripping off his tie, Mac flung it aside, not caring that it fluttered to the floor. "If the job is what this evening is all about, forget it."

"The reservations are made. We have our special table in the corner by the waterfall." Jennifer clipped diamonds to her earlobes, and adjusted the drape of a designer gown before lifting her eyes to the mirror. "Daddy's expecting us."

"The reservations are always made. Always at the same table, and Daddy's always waiting." Mac glared at her reflection. Even with lingerie the blue silk left little to the imagination. For once he was immune. "We aren't going.

The reservations can be canceled, or your father can use them alone.''

"We?" Jennifer bristled at the assumption she wouldn't go if he didn't.

"All right, then, *I! I'm* not going."

Final touches complete, with her hands clasped before her, Jennifer strove to keep her voice steady. "You could listen to what he has to offer."

"No, I can't. Not again. I've done nothing but listen to the two of you for months. I've tried to get you, at least, to hear me. I'm an engineer. I belong in the field. I could never in a million years be a desk jockey. I appreciate your father's offer, but it's not for me."

"This wonderful endeavor in South America is?" She sounded like a shrew, but was too angry to care.

Mac's fists were clenched, but his voice was more restrained than it had been in dozens of arguments before. "As a matter of fact, yes. It's a marvelous opportunity with an outstanding company. I was fortunate to be singled out by them. But more than the honor and opportunity, it's something I want to do."

"At half the salary my father is offering."

"Perhaps even less, but it's enough."

"For whom?" Jennifer demanded, her nails scoring the backs of her hands.

"For us."

"If I want to continue living like this." A broad gesture dismissed the tiny two-room apartment.

"It suited you when we were married." Mac's voice was quiet now, from anger so fierce it must be controlled at all cost.

"You mean when I seduced you, don't you? When I was so certain our differences would never hurt us."

"I said what I meant, Jennifer. You were happy here for more than that one night."

"So I was happy here," she conceded. "It was adequate for a while, but not forever."

"Six months isn't forever."

"It didn't have to be this long. We could have taken the house Daddy wanted to give us as a wedding present."

"We couldn't afford it, or the servants it would have required, or the membership at the country club that came with it. Or the Roadster that would have looked so handsome in its drive." Mac abandoned sarcasm for reason. "Hell, Jennifer, I couldn't afford the insurance on a Mercedes."

"None of it would have cost you a penny."

"Money isn't the issue. It never was."

"Pride," Jennifer spat. "We have to live like paupers because of your selfish pride?" She didn't understand his obsession with ego. How his sense of worth depended on his own accomplishments and with being his own man.

"We've had times here I'll never forget. We've loved and we've laughed and we've been comfortable. It isn't what you grew up with, but it isn't a hovel."

"You're saving the hovels for South America."

Mac sighed and picked up his tie. "For the tenth time, there are settlements near the site. Some are resort villages with nearly all the amenities you've missed here."

"And starving children begging on street corners."

"The people are poor. That's the reason for the project. To harness the river for power, to bring cleaner water and better roads, and a chance at prosperity. Then maybe their hungry children wouldn't offend you by begging on the street."

Jennifer stood mute in her finery, her perfect evening in shambles. She had been so sure Mac would abandon the idea of the South American project. But pride, ego, anger, wouldn't let him. Unnerved by the fear that she really might lose him, she tried again to dissuade him. "If you love me, you won't leave me."

"I'm not leaving you. I'm asking you to go with me. Graduation is less than a week away, and you've shown no interest in work or a career, so there's nothing to keep you here. I need this project, Jennifer. We both need it if our marriage is to survive. Forget you're Edwin Burke's daughter and be my wife. Come with me."

Jennifer was very still; tears gathered in her eyes. "You've taken the job already, haven't you?"

"I told you weeks ago. You refused to listen. We're scheduled to leave in two weeks."

"*We?* There is no we, Mac. If you go, you go alone."

He was suddenly pale, his face gaunt, the tension aging him. His chest rose as if his body were starved for air. Then slowly his shoulders bowed. "There's nothing I can say to persuade you?"

"I won't live in a strange country. I couldn't bear the children with eyes too big for their faces, and bodies too heavy for matchstick arms and legs." Even to Jennifer the remark was cruel and callous, but it was too late to take it back.

"I never thought it would come to this."

After weeks of discord and rage, it seemed unreal that a marriage could end so succinctly. "Differences," she murmured, and in a word explained everything.

"You'll handle the legalities?"

"A divorce?"

"If it's what you want, Jennifer. Desertion should suffice."

She turned away, unable to face him. After a moment she whispered, "I'll see to it. As soon as possible you'll have your freedom and your name. I don't want either." Her body straightened, her shoulders were taut. "My father's waiting, I'll leave you to your packing."

That simply, a marriage died and she never saw him again.

A tap on her door drew Jennifer from the past. Sally Brown, her secretary, advanced a step into the office. "Dr. McLachlan?"

Sliding back her chair, Jennifer rose. "Yes, Sally?"

"Chrissie's parents are waiting in the lobby."

"Ask them to come up."

Sally hesitated. "Dr. McLachlan, we all know how difficult this is for you." Another hesitation, then a flustered rush. "We know, too, how lucky our patients and their parents are to have you." Her comment made, Sally hurried away, leaving Jennifer alone again.

The sound of the rain disturbed the quiet, drawing her back to the window. With the approach of evening, the day had grown grayer. The silver mist of afternoon had become an ugly wintry fog blanketing the panes, blurring her vision like the tears that had fallen for Chrissie. For herself. For Mac.

"Mac." If only... Jennifer shook her head. It did no good to wish. He'd walked out of her life nearly ten years ago. She hadn't believed he would go. To the very end, she'd waited for a call that never came. Instead, with that strange, quiet rage seething within him, coping with a hurt too deep to heal, he had simply made her cease to exist for him.

But if the stranger in the rain was Mac?

"No!" With her fist she tapped the window, feeling the cold that touched her soul. "But if he was?"

"Dr. McLachlan?"

Spinning from the window, escaping her thoughts, Jennifer faced the couple who stood in the door. Even if she hadn't been expecting them, she would have recognized them. From the pain etched in their faces. Because Chrissie was a carbon copy of her mother.

"Mr. and Mrs. Hanyon, please, come in." With hands outstretched, she went to comfort them.

Jennifer spent the next day assuring herself that Robert Bruce McLachlan had no part in the initial plans for the new hospital wing. She spent a week convincing herself she had only imagined the familiarity of the stranger in the rain.

The second week, when her heart was finally at peace again, when she left the hospital at the end of a day that stretched into evening, he was waiting by her car.

Two

___

Garish yellow light spilled over pitch black asphalt, distorting as much as it revealed. A flimsy illusion of protection from dangers lurking in the night. With her head down, her shoulders hunched against a cold that seemed colder after the unseasonably warm weeks before, Jennifer was not thinking of danger, or the leaden quiet of night. Her footsteps traced their path by rote, taking her weary body where they would, leaving her mind to wrestle with the problems of her day.

She had no warning. No sixth sense whispered. Only the scuff of a shifting shoe betrayed his presence a half-drawn breath before his quiet voice reached out to her.

"Working a little late, aren't you, Doc?"

Jennifer halted in midstride, her foot coming down in place with a jolt. The briefcase she carried slipped unheeded from slack fingers. Her head came up, and she stared blindly into an unnatural glare. Ironically, she was startled more than frightened as eyes adjusted, focused, and a bearish shape materialized out of a white haze. A man, cloaked in a bulky parka, as changed as the voice, yet as familiar.

"Mac."

He pushed away from the side of a nondescript gray car, his look on the surface nonchalant, as if late-night meetings in wintry parking lots were common.

As if ten years hadn't passed, and a broken marriage had never been.

"Hello, Jennifer." A slight hint of Scotland was still there. A legacy from the grandmother he'd never known, passed on by Dare, the older brother he adored.

Mac. Once Jennifer had lain in his arms, listening to his words, imagining a boy worshiping the man who was the center of his universe. Walking as he walked, speaking as he spoke, unconsciously absorbing nuances of a land he'd never seen.

Whispered words, lilting, in Gaelic accents. Words of love.

Now her heart lay as stone in her chest. While blood drained from her face, a thousand sensations clawed at her, a thousand memories. One after the other, too swiftly, too powerful. A mad kaleidoscope too mad to comprehend. She was voiceless as he took a step and then another, moving closer.

"We meet again, Jennifer." Then softly, "Or should I say, Dr. McLachlan?"

For an unguarded moment there was anger in his face, in his voice—anger as new and as raw as her memories. As if it was only yesterday she'd angrily declared she wanted nothing from him. Not his love, nor their marriage. Not his name.

"Should I, Jennifer?"

The question hung between them, more complicated than it seemed. Needing an answer for more than a name. An answer she couldn't give. Deliberately misunderstanding, she gave surface recognition to his question. "If you wish."

"Ahh, if I wish." He took another step, a fierce look blazing in his eyes. When she moved back, an instinct she couldn't suppress, he moved with her, neatly hemming her between his body and her car. "I wish a lot of things, *Dr. McLachlan.*" Bracing his hands against the top of the car, he completed her prison. "I've wondered how it would be if our paths crossed again. The lovely Jennifer Burke's and mine. It wasn't beyond the realm of possibility. A native Atlantan and a blue-collar guy whose work and contacts take him in and out of the city. Not a likely coincidence, but not impossible.''

"Your work? In Barclay?" A chill February wind nipped at her face, stinging her pale cheeks with color, teasing her hair from the scarf tied at her nape. Brushing a wayward strand from her eyes, she met the hot blue stare. "Rick said your life's work was in South America. That one project led to another, hardly allowing time for visits home in between."

Summarily dismissing her curiosity, he moved closer, so close his body brushed hers. "Forget South America. It's not important at the moment." His gaze narrowed, roaming her face, as if the answers he wanted could be found there.

A light flickered, an engine droned to a stop. The first arrival for the weekend shift, covering Friday midnight, to Monday morning at eight. In the fleeting distraction Jennifer bowed her head, shielding her face from his probing gaze. Her throat was dry, her body cramped with tension. Long after the singular headlamps were extinguished, bolts of light flashed in a storm behind her eyes.

A warning to which she couldn't pay the respect it commanded. Not now. Not yet. "Mac, this isn't the time for explanations."

"Isn't it?"

"Midnight in a parking lot? You know it isn't."

"Then when?"

"I'm not sure any time would be right." Her voice was steady, pleasing her with its calm. A calm she knew was tenuous at best. "Do explanations really matter anymore?"

Mac laughed, a short humorless growl. "I come home after nearly ten years and discover the woman who never bothered to divorce me still bears my name, and you don't think I deserve an explanation?" He turned her face to his. "No, Jennifer," he muttered. "You aren't getting off that easily."

"Mac..." A second car drove into the lot, a second engine died. The thud of heavy doors accompanied the sound of animated conversation.

Mac straightened, his body moving away from hers, yet he didn't release her. His gaze never wavered. With his thumb he traced the bruised circles of fatigue under her eyes. He felt the clammy cold of her skin. The third shift was arriving, Jennifer was just leaving. She'd worked a sixteen-hour day. "You're right, this isn't the time or the place, and you're exhausted."

If Jennifer meant to draw a breath of relief, his next words had it catching in her throat. Not certain she understood, she blurted out, "I beg your pardon?"

"Do you? Perhaps you should tell me later for what. Now, give me your keys," he repeated.

Any shred of calm had flown. She was frantic to move away from the car and out of the circle of his arms, but the adrenaline that had kept her going through two shifts deserted her. Instead, she leaned against the door, hoping she could muster enough indignation that he would just go away. "You must be out of your mind. Why would I give you my keys?"

Mac smiled, a cynical quirk of his lips. "I may very well be out of my mind. But I still want your keys to drive you home."

Astonishment stirred a bit of the faltering adrenaline. "Why the devil would you want to drive me home?"

"Because, from the look of you, you won't make it alone."

"I've worked extra shifts before. I've been tired before. And somehow I've made it home without your help."

His gaze swept over her face, dwelling on heavy lidded eyes with darkness gathering like purple shadows beneath them. He'd seen stronger men dead on their feet from exhaustion less apparent. "Have you, Jennifer?" He asked with a new note of gentleness. "Have you ever been this tired before?"

Jennifer couldn't deny the truth. She couldn't remember when fatigue had been so unrelenting. Not even years ago when her life was in disaster and there was no one to turn to.

"A rough two weeks." She tried to shrug away too many sleepless nights obsessed with a stranger in the rain. Too many worries. Too many heartaches. Being thirty instead of twenty.

"Too rough," Mac said curtly, stating the obvious.

"So? Why would you care?"

"I'm damned if I know, Jennifer." His hand was extended, palm up, waiting. Implacable. "Give me your keys."

She hadn't the stamina to argue. So long as she got home, she didn't care who did or didn't drive. She didn't care how he planned to get back to his lodgings. He could walk or find a cab. His choice. His problem. If he could find his way between South America and Backwoods, Carolina, he could manage in a tiny town on the outskirts of Atlanta. Taking her keys from the pocket of her blazer, rasping out her address, she tossed them to him.

Without a word Mac caught them, scooped up her fallen briefcase and, with his hand at her elbow, tucked her into the passenger seat of her car. Any comment he might have made about the not-so-new, but prudent American-made car, was silenced as she sighed quietly, leaning back into the seat.

As soon as her head touched she was asleep. For the first time Mac could examine her unnoticed by prying eyes. He could see for himself, without the embellishment of rumor and gossip, what ten years had done to her.

When he'd signed on as consultant for the project he'd no knowledge that Jennifer was part of the hospital staff. No inkling she'd become more than her father's pampered darling. He'd come to do a job. No more. Though he was not a part of the crew, he shared sporadically in their camaraderie. At first he'd paid no attention to the flirtations rife between hospital staff and construction crew. Nor to the chatter that accompanied them.

He'd been hearing the name McLachlan for days before he listened. Dr. McLachlan this. Dr. McLachlan that. The name ran like a constant thread through so many moving stories. She was a kind woman, a giving woman. A paragon too good to be true.

Then, in some innocent emphasis, Dr. McLachlan became Jennifer. Mac heard. Then he listened.

Dr. Jennifer McLachlan? The idea was staggering. He tried to fit the Jennifer he'd known into the mold of the woman whose name seemed to be on every tongue. Failing miserably, he dismissed it as a great coincidence.

He *tried* to dismiss it. Jennifer wouldn't stay dismissed.

First he found himself listening greedily. Then came the questions, spilling out of him like a broken logjam.

How old was Jennifer McLachlan? How tall? How beautiful?

Heaven help him, every answer was without flaw. Everything fit.

Dr. Jennifer McLachlan was thirty, give or take a year. She stood five-feet-three. This time give or take a fraction. She was blond, brown-eyed, with a good figure, if a little too thin. A quiet lady totally dedicated to her work.

Mac had clung stubbornly to his belief that the names and similarities were coincidences. In his wildest imagining he couldn't reconcile the hardworking professional with the woman who was his wife.

Doubt prompted his last question. The answer left him sleepless for days.

Jennifer McLachlan had been married. No one knew what happened to the marriage, or to her husband. With the last, Mac's source paused, regarded him speculatively, noted the similarity of their names, wondered aloud at Mac's unusual interest and, with a suspicious gleam, fell silent.

Mac hadn't confirmed or denied, letting speculations and suspicions lie. He still wasn't ready to believe.

Finding himself a target of conjecture, he retreated, listening for each mention of her name, filing it away, never questioning again. Careful to draw as little attention to himself as possible, he began to watch the parking lot at shift change. A useless exercise. The small blond physician arrived early and left late. She was almost never in the scheduled melee.

Then one rare day she was among the rush. Small, bright, her hair shining golden in the winter sun. From the usual departing banter a chorus of laughter rose. One melodic, distinct, with an underlying note of melancholy.

Jennifer's laugh. Not even sadness and the changes wrought by years had changed it.

Pieces of a surprising puzzle had fallen into place. With everything but the answers. It was the consuming need to have those answers that had drawn him to her tonight.

Watching the sleeping woman, he saw the tension ease from the rigid lines of her body. Her face was half-turned toward him. Security lamps shining through the windshield marked every feature in harsh relief. But even in that unkind light he could see that with the passage of time she'd grown lovelier.

Mac watched, fascinated, as sleep erased her cares. Brows drawn down by stress and driving determination arched undisturbed by frowns and pain. Her lashes lay thick and golden over smooth, flawless skin. Her face was thinner than when he'd met her so many years ago. Each feature more defined, the classic bone structure more apparent. There was maturity in the sweep of her brow, strength in the jut of her chin and quiet sophistication in the delicate shadows curving beneath high cheekbones.

Only her mouth was unchanged. Her lips were full, pouting like a young girl waiting to be kissed.

But Jennifer was a woman, not a young girl. She wanted nothing from him. Yet after ten years she was still his wife, she still bore his name. Mac turned the key in the ignition, and wondered why?

"Can I get you something? A drink? Coffee?"

Keys still in hand, Mac swung about, shifting his attention from the curiously bare room to Jennifer. She stood by the door clutching her coat, a careworn waif, functioning on pure willpower. "I didn't come here to add the trouble of playing hostess to your day, Jennifer."

Why had he come? The question streaked through her mind. Another she wasn't ready to deal with.

"No trouble," she said with a casualness that sounded false even to her. When he'd shown no sign of leaving her at her door, she'd had no choice but to ask him in. An untenable situation. Making coffee or pouring a drink would be busywork for hand and mind.

Hanging his parka along with her blazer on the coat tree by the door, she moved from the hall to the kitchen, part of a large, single room that served many functions. A simple room even in its multipurposes and completely to her liking.

Not bothering to hide his interest, he let his gaze follow her. She was apprehensive and, under his scrutiny, grew worse. Tension was back in the set of her shoulders. Her eyes were restless, darting warily toward him, then quickly away. In the close quarters of her home, she seemed claustrophobic. As if she would fly apart at the least provocation. When she turned to the sink to fill a pot with water, the muscles of her neck, glimpsed beneath the fall of her hair, were knotted and tight.

Dropping her keys in a basket by the door, he crossed to her, his footsteps quiet over quarry tiles. When he laid a hand on her shoulder she didn't jerk away, but her body became stone. "I didn't come to be entertained." Ignoring her resistance, he took the pot from her, setting it aside and turning her toward him. When fear leapt into her eyes, he cursed his clumsy approach. His voice roughened with anger. "Dammit! I didn't come to attack you, either."

"I didn't think you did."

Despite her denial, watchfulness was still in her eyes. "Then tell me why you're afraid, Jennifer."

"I'm not afraid." Another denial. Too quick. Too intense.

"No?" Raising his hand from her arm to her face, he brushed a stray lock from her temple. When she recoiled from his touch, he let his hand drop, his point taken.

Needing space, Jennifer tried to back away and found no way out. The rim of the counter pressed hard against her spine. Retreat was impossible. Her only defense was offense. And anger. "Look, Mac." Her chin was set, her scowl fierce. "You can't just waltz into my life in the dead of night after all these years and expect me to act as if nothing has changed."

"Not everything has."

A quiver of alarm ran through her. Did he sense the wariness was more than fear? Did those intense blue eyes see the ache of bittersweet memories made more poignant by the touch of his strong, hard hands? Did he know how profoundly their few short months together had changed her life? He couldn't. She was second-guessing, reading into his words more significance than they could have.

Toying absently with the scarf at the nape of her neck, she chose to dissemble. "I don't know what you mean, or think you mean. After so long, everything has changed."

"It isn't a matter of thinking, Jennifer." The line of his mouth was resolute. He wouldn't be denied. "You know exactly what I mean."

"All right!" she snapped, sucking in a long, steadying breath. "I suppose you're referring to our marriage."

His expression didn't change. "An astute supposition, Doc, but you're still hedging."

Her fingers curled around the knotted scarf. Pain exploded in the base of her skull, spiraling to the top of her head in excruciating, thought-shattering waves. And every warning she'd tried to ignore exacted its particular due. Migraine. From too many long hours beneath fluorescent lights, breathing too long the suffocating, lung-searing reek of the hospital. Facing stress heaped upon stress. Heartache upon heartache.

Pain. Primal. Obscene. A netherworld.

Robber of dignity.

A rarity.

Her vision blurred. Her pretense of anger died. Clenching her teeth, despising the weakness, despairing that it should come now, she concentrated solely on getting through the remainder of his stay with some dignity. Clinging to the last paltry shreds of her strength, she conceded grimly. "You're wondering about a divorce that never happened."

Mac waited, not giving an inch.

Jennifer closed her eyes. A mistake. The dizzying darkness was too inviting. She wanted to curl into it. To hide from the pain in her head and the pain from her past. Folly.

Her past was standing before her, demanding explanations for the present.

She struggled to clear her thoughts, gathering fading energy. With her eyes open she addressed the inevitable and prayed it was enough. "You're wondering why I still carry your name."

"Bingo!" Mac caught back a shudder of relief. His name. He'd wanted to hear her say it. He needed it. Too intent on Jennifer's motives to wonder at his own, he probed for more. "Now that you're through fencing, perhaps you'll tell me why, Jennifer."

The name. All he knew of was the name. Relief was a tiny, flickering light that even the darkness of her silent storm could not quench. But neither could that small light chase away the storm. Jennifer bowed her head, summoning her courage.

"Why Dr. McLachlan?" he asked almost conversationally, but making himself clear. "Why not Dr. Burke?"

Jennifer heard the uncompromising determination. He would have his answer. Then she could be alone. Lifting her head to face his questions, she found he was only a form. A towering black column in the morass of a ghastly rainbow. When he spoke again his words pulsed in her brain. A distorted, muddled echo she had to think to decipher. And thinking hurt.

Something of her confusion was in her look. A look that had him making explanations he hadn't intended. "I won't tell you that I didn't know the marriage was still intact. But it was a shock learning you kept my name. I wonder about your change of heart, Jennifer."

Change of heart. Words. A turn of phrase, penetrating her daze as effectively as a blow. Jennifer remembered two hearts. One broken. One tiny and delicate, which couldn't be changed.

God help her, she had to get through this. Had to give him partial truths, and make him believe. Rousing from her leaden somnolence, forcing the searing torment to the recesses of her mind, she reached for the composure to convince. "There's no mystery, Mac. At first I couldn't believe it was truly ending as it was, that you would leave me.'' With a self-condemning shrug she turned her back to him.

Above the counter, in an obvious place of honor, hung a childish drawing framed in plain, dark walnut. A mass of lines and colors scrawled across fading construction paper, an indistinguishable subject. The attempt of a very young hand at drawing trees and the sun? A doorless, windowless house topped by a yellow roof? Perhaps, he surmised, even flowers?

As her gaze raised to it, Mac remembered other childish favors he'd glimpsed gathered in scattered clusters throughout the room. Grouped without rhyme or apparent reason, but together. This one stood alone. A drawing cherished above many. Drawn by a most special patient among all her special patients?

He wondered who. He wondered why.

Then there was no time for wondering as her voice reached past his thoughts, stirring old memories.

''I was the golden girl, remember? My world was a perfect place, where nothing but beauty was allowed. Its inhabitants waited to grant my every wish. Nothing bad could ever happen, and no one I loved would ever leave me.''

Her hand moved from her nape to her temple, her palm brushing hard against it as if brushing away some irritant. Despite the agitation in her actions, her voice was steady and calm. So calm it concerned him, but still he waited.

Jennifer was grateful only for the willpower that allowed her to continue. ''By the time I realized how wrong I was, that my life had not come with guarantees, my perfect world had crumbled. Then none of it seemed to matter anymore. Not your leaving, or the divorce. Or even taking back my name.

''I thought the day would come when you would want your freedom, and there would be time enough for the divorce then.'' She shrugged again, and pain she'd carefully tucked away escaped like an animal caged too long. A hand flew to her temple, then to her nape. The other gripped the counter. Her voice was a whisper. ''After a while, I didn't think about it anymore.''

Mac knew something was wrong. This was more than re-action to his prodding. Taking her by the shoulders, aware on another level of how fragile she was, he turned her to him. Her honey-brown eyes were too dark in her pale face. Her unfocused stare looked through him. "Jennifer? What's wrong?"

"It's nothing." The lie erupted from her.

"Nothing!"

Through a roar in her ears she heard the panic in his voice, and felt a need to reassure him. "A migraine. I should've…" She stopped, losing her train of thought, then remembered that he was worried. "Only a migraine."

Only! He didn't know whether to laugh or curse her min-imizing diagnosis. He chose to act, instead. "What can I do?" He didn't release her, but his grip at her shoulders eased. "Is there something you take?"

"Something…"

"Tell me what. Tell me where." Accustomed to com-mand, Mac's reaction was natural.

"I can do it." Jennifer laid a hand on his chest, intend-ing to step past him, and ended clutching at him. "Sorry," she tried a smile. "A little dizzy."

"More than a little." Her fingers, still twined in his shirt, were shaking. He felt their tremor against his chest. "Come sit at the table while I find what you need."

"I can manage." Despite her protest, Jennifer didn't move. She didn't dare.

"I'm sure you can," Mac said. "But I'm here, Jennifer, and you don't have to."

She didn't argue as he walked with her to the table. She was even grateful when he listened carefully to her spare description of the medication she needed and its location in a bathroom cabinet. When he patted her shoulder as if she would break from more than a trace of his touch and promised to be only a minute, she managed what she thought was a smile. Watching his broad back disappear down the hall, she didn't consider the strangeness of Mac's presence in her home, or wonder anymore why he was there. She simply closed her eyes and let the pain come.

In white, blinding lights it washed over her. A raging tide, pounding, stabbing. She didn't hear her moan borne on a long-held sigh, nor his desperate curse and the rush of his booted footsteps that followed. She was riding the crest of agony now. A second was an hour. A minute, a lifetime.

She ceased to think. She simply existed.

Mac paused at the door of her bedroom, orienting himself, before striding through the Spartan room. The bath, like her bedroom, was strictly utilitarian. And like the bedroom the decor was minimal, the lines simple, giving it a classic style of its own. Her house, or what he'd seen of it, was the same. A place for living, with no unnecessary trappings for show. Yet the result was pleasing, comfortable in its simplicity.

The cabinet she'd directed him to exhibited the same order. The medication she described was exactly where he expected. Taking the small vial from its niche, he reflected that the order about her was more than the natural product of an analytical intelligence. Order could be the only means of survival for a life and mind in constant chaos.

If her work produced such great turmoil that these stringent measures were needed to counteract it, why had she chosen it?

The woman he'd known would not have.

Closing the cabinet, he chided himself for loitering, even though he hadn't. Neither a second nor a move had been wasted. What he'd seen, the conclusion he'd drawn, were from an ambience absorbed, rather than from time-consuming study.

Returning to the room of all purposes, he went to her side. Her head was clasped between her hands, giving the impression that, were they vices, she would exert the greatest pressure possible.

He touched her, signaling his return. She moved her hands away, but didn't acknowledge him. Her face was a chalky mask of colorless lips and deepening lines. She looked frail huddled over the table. Too frail.

He saw the throbbing pulse at her temple, remembering how she'd brushed at it. Brushing away the pain? "Jennifer, I have the medication, but first I'm going to put you to bed."

She didn't object. He didn't give her the option. As carefully as he could, he lifted her in his arms, aware too late that every jolt and every step was punishment. "Ahh, damn," he murmured as her body clenched and she bit back a ragged groan. "I'm sorry, I didn't mean to hurt you."

Her arms were looped loosely about him, her head tucked into his shoulder. Her lips moved against the curve of his neck. He thought he heard her say, "I know."

The journey to her bedroom seemed to take forever, but only because he knew his mistake and regretted every move. For what good it did his conscience, each step was taken as carefully as treading through broken glass. At her bedside he felt a profound sense of relief. Half kneeling, half bending, he sat her down, letting the pillows cushion and elevate her head. He knew that lying prone would add to her vertigo.

Her skin was cool and clammy, and he searched out something to serve as cover. Then he thought again, rationally, not with his heart. As with lying down, it was better that she be too cool than overheated. And she should have her medication.

"Should've had them before Sir Galahad went into his act." He wouldn't dwell on his mistake. What was done couldn't be undone. He knelt by her. "Jennifer, your tablets. How many should you have?"

"One." She didn't stir from the pillows or open her eyes.

The tiny white pellet astonished him. Could anything so small deal with the misery he saw? "Only one?"

"One."

When the tablet was in her palm, he climbed to his feet. "I'll get a glass of water."

"No water." While he stood irresolutely, she explained in a tight voice, "Sublingual." Then, grinding it out, reassurance spaced between cautious breaths, "Thank you. For coming. I'll be fine. Five minutes. All I need is five—"

"Shh." He stopped her. "Just rest. I'm not going anywhere." An unexpected thought disturbed him. "Unless there's someone I should call. Someone you need."

"No one."

"Plans for the weekend?"

"Nothing." She was drifting, not bothering to fight, letting the hurt ebb and flow within her. Then the tablet beneath her tongue began its sorcery, and with each beat of her heart the migraine diminished. Each infinite degree a blessing.

Five minutes, a lifetime. Jennifer thanked God it would only take that.

Mac was worried, restless, feeling like a great hulking fool. Worse, a voyeur. He needed to move. He dared not. The quiet tranquility of the room made him clumsy, an interloper disrupting its harmony. More than that, he feared any motion would disturb her. What should he do? He couldn't leave, yet he didn't want to hover. He wouldn't intrude more than he had already, as she fought her private battle.

Compromising, he sat in a chair by the terrace door, taking a stack of magazines from a nearby table. Regrettably, they were medical publications. Nevertheless, thumbing through them, he settled down to wait.

Four minutes. Three and a half. Three.

Her bedside clock with its bright digital numerals moved in slow motion. He would be stupid to think five minutes was the exact time, but he watched the clock ticking off endless seconds and listened to the stillness. He hadn't been this helpless since he'd walked away from her.

A vow, made that day, that he would not be, had never been broken.

Until now.

Weary with the pretense of reading, he put the magazines away. What was it about Jennifer, either Jennifer, that shattered promises he'd spent so long guarding? He should have learned from college, when he'd been so blinded by her that he'd gone into a relationship that every shred of judgment warned was wrong. Yet here he was again, a lot older, he would've thought wiser, and one trill of sad laughter, one vulnerable look, and every bit of common sense was swept away. Every vow forgotten.

But only until she was better, and he had the answers he'd come for.

"Mac."

He bolted out of his chair, startled by her voice. She was sitting on the side of the bed with her feet on the floor.

Her dark gaze met his. "I thought I'd dreamed you."

"I'm real, very real."

"I remember. You wanted to know..."

"It doesn't matter now." Crossing the room, he knelt before her. There were no roses in her cheeks, but her color was better. Laying the back of his hand against her forehead, he found her skin still cool, but not clammy. "How do you feel?"

"Fuzzy." She wrinkled her nose at the description. "Aware of every part of my body. As if my hair is a weight on my skull and my fingernails too heavy for my fingertips. My heart is too monotonous, my breath too loud." At his look of consternation, she explained, "the medication, its aftereffects." Her fingers curled over his wrist. "Most of all I feel stupid."

"Because of the migraine?"

"And the weakness."

"I haven't seen any weakness, Jennifer."

"You're being kind."

"Kindness isn't one of my better traits."

"I remember when it was." Sliding her fingertips from his throbbing pulse, she refuted his denial. "I think it is still. More than you would have me know."

Mac dragged a hand through his hair, struggling to ignore old feelings stirred by her words. The leap of remembered passion licked at him in a ravenous flame. Ten years! Time for memories to be forgotten.

Time enough for desire to die.

"These headaches—" his voice was laced with all he wanted to forget "—how often do they occur?"

"Seldom."

"Define seldom."

"Before today, only one, seven years ago."

"But bad enough that you never forgot it." He gestured at the vial on a bedside table. "Why else would you have these?"

"Once burned." She let the cliché drift away as she fumbled with the scarf at her neck. Even its negligible weight was too much with the heightened awareness. Her efforts were awkward, ineffectual.

Mac drew her hands away, dealing with the scarf himself. Tucking the bit of scarlet in a shirt pocket, he combed his fingers through her hair until it lay bright and unrestrained over her shoulders. Once he'd been fascinated by her hair, reveling in the brush of it over his body as he made love to her.

Once.

He stroked her cheek, his skin warm against hers, comforting. Her downcast gaze lifted to his, the echo of hurt and gratitude still in them. It was the most natural thing, then, to kiss her. To touch her mouth with his. To brush her lips with his lips, soothing, offering solace.

Jennifer accepted his kiss, his comfort and solace. Pain was forgotten. Even the years that separated them. Her mouth softened under his, giving as much as taking. Asking nothing.

Slowly Mac drew away, watching as her lashes fluttered against her cheeks. He traced the blue ribbon of a vein that still pulsed at her temple, lingered. "Jennifer..."

Abruptly, aware of what he'd done, what was happening to him, he recoiled from her, his hands fisted, his face bleak. He hadn't intended this. He didn't want her. Didn't need her. "I should go." Rising, he stood looking down at her. A strong woman, a beautiful woman. "You'll be all right alone?"

She hadn't moved. The only change was the beginning of a flush of color darkening exquisite cheekbones. "I've been alone for a long time."

He heard no censure, no self-pity, only the facing of reality. Nodding, he turned away. He was stepping through the doorway into the hall when she stopped him.

"Mac?"

He turned, not sure what to expect.

"Thank you, for what you've done for me."

"It was the least I could do."

"For anyone, right?"

"Right." He turned away.

"Mac."

He stood in the shadow of the hall.

"You were right."

He waited for an explanation of the cryptic remark. When there was none, he left her. Without a question. Without answers. Without a backward glance.

Three

———

"**Y**o! McLachlan."

Mac looked up from a string of numbers he'd been staring at without comprehension. "Yeah, Tiny? What do you want?"

Billy Stratton, better known as Tiny, dropped the last few feet from a scaffold, landing agilely on massive booted feet. His grin was a flash of white in his permanently weather-burned face. "Thought you'd like to know—your lady's arriving."

Mac pushed back his hard hat and tucked the folded papers into the back pocket of his jeans, buying time. "My what?"

"Your lady." Tiny's eyes were dancing. "You know, the one you're always asking about, the good-looking little doc."

"I'm not always asking, and she's not my lady."

"Sure about that?" Tiny leaned against a steel column and pushed back his own hat, exposing a shock of nearly white hair. "Seein' as both you and the doc have been married, and you're so interested in her, I've been speculating you might be star-crossed lovers."

"Star-crossed lovers?" Mac laughed, pretending the story was ridiculous. "The rumor mill has been working overtime, and you've been listening, I see."

Tiny was watching him with a look of dawning surprise. Tiny loved gossip, didn't believe a word of it, but loved it, anyway. Now the gossip was suddenly credible. "The names are the same, the ages right. So is the math. Doc's husband has been out of the picture for years. You haven't been in the country for just as long.

"Makes a good story and solves a puzzle." Sliding his hat an inch farther, Tiny drawled, "You aren't exactly denying anything."

A crane ready to lift steel from the floor of the construction site roared into life. If Mac had wanted to reply he couldn't. Better, he decided, to leave it alone than to lie.

Tiny Stratton, senior member of the crew, had become Mac's closet friend and wasn't ready to let it drop. Moving away from the steel, he strolled past Mac, and at the last minute, he stopped. Almost casually, he shouted over the din of the monstrous engine, "Was I a McLachlan and that was my lady, I'd be makin' a move to get her back. Doc's for damn sure a fine-looking woman." Then, after a pause for emphasis, "Even if she docs look a might peaked this morning."

It took every ounce of his strength to keep from taking the bait. Every muscle protested his effort not to spin in his tracks and see for himself. Instead, Mac lifted a quizzical brow. "Does she now?"

"Just a mite." Tiny chucked him under the chin, an unlikely mother hen making a point to a wayward chick. "Not as peaked as you."

Tiny's disappointment that his ploy hadn't worked would have been funny if Mac had felt like laughing. He only shrugged and let it lie.

"Guess Doc had herself one ripsnortin' weekend. The sort that leaves you queasy on Monday."

"I guess."

Tiny rolled his eyes. Blood from a turnip was easier than a rise from Mac. "You wouldn't know anything about it?"

"Not a thing, Billy." Billy, not Tiny, a small formality setting boundaries. The blast of the crane was louder. Conversation, difficult already, became impossible. "Since we both have better things to do with our time than stand here shouting down the machinery, let's let it go at that." Mac formed the last with his mouth, no sound issued from his throat. It would have been a waste to try.

Tiny shrugged, but was not quite defeated. With a too-innocent expression he glanced past Mac to the hospital parking lot, flashed a knowing grin and trudged away.

Mac was left to wonder what this man, with his face burned to mahogany by the sun and carved by wind, knew. Or thought he knew.

Tiny was halfway across the site, giving handwritten instructions to the operator of the yellow crane before Mac let himself turn. Before he let his hungry eyes search the lot for some glimpse of her.

Too late. No one stood near the dependable gray car. No one crossed the wintry asphalt lot. Jennifer had disappeared into the cavernous maw of the hospital. Only she and the Fates knew when she would emerge again.

Mac tucked his hand into the breast pocket of his parka. A fold of scarlet silk was soft to his rough fingers. He hadn't discovered the forgotten bit of whimsy until he'd flagged down a cab a block from her house. His first inclination had been to turn the cabbie around. To return the bright scrap and see for himself if she was all right. His second was to toss it out the window, discarding it, forgetting it and the woman who'd worn it.

He'd done neither. Stroking the ribbon of scarlet, abraded skin catching at the fine threads, he'd paced the small space of his quarters, seeing Jennifer in his mind's eye. Hearing her voice in the silence. Her blouse had been red. As red as the scarf. Her skirt, slim and black, her nylons dark and sheer, her shoes sensible. She'd worn only a watch, no other jewelry. Not even a ring.

He'd forgotten how small she was until he held her in his arms, how her voice was a throb of music even in distress.

He'd gone to the telephone time and again over the weekend wanting to hear her voice. Needing to know that she had recovered. Each time he'd backed away, reminding himself that all he wanted or needed from her was answers.

And she'd given them. Quiet, concise, reasonable answers that left just enough unsaid to leave him confounded and troubled, and frankly curious.

Curiosity? Was the word strong enough for the need that was becoming obsession. And why, after so long, should it concern him? Any of it?

No matter how he asked himself, no matter that he had no explanation, nothing changed. He'd prowled and paced, then prowled some more. She was always in his mind, whispering *I know,* to his claim that he hadn't meant to hurt her. His voice had been harsh, hers a whisper against his throat.

A sound he couldn't forget, leaving the feeling she meant far more than he understood. When he was sure his mind was playing tricks, making something of nothing, her last words echoed through his thoughts.

You were right.

When? Years ago? In their lost years? Now?

Restless hours had brought him no closer to resolution.

"Curiosity killed the cat," he grumbled now to the sound of the crane. "The tomcat too."

"Hey, Mac." Tiny's heavy hand fell on his shoulder, his bullhorn voice booming as pandemonium quieted. "I just happen to know that the little blonde you're not interested in takes a break in the canteen at the hospital at nine. Usually grabs a cup of juice and a cracker of some sort, or yogurt." He didn't even pretend to glance at his watch to check the time. "Should be there in twenty minutes or so. Not that you're interested, of course, but I thought you might like to know."

Mac didn't bother with pretending again, either. There was no use trying with this new and fast friend who saw and heard everything that went on around him. "Thanks, Tiny."

"Anytime."

"See you." Mac walked to the construction office. He would discard his hard hat, comb his hair and wash the inevitable grime from his face. No need in turning the lady off before he could make his move. An hour or two over dinner and one more question or two should fill in the blanks. Then this chapter of a dreary saga could be closed, and he could get on with a life put on hold for too long.

"Mac."

"Yo?" He swung around to face Tiny.

"Just one thing. When you get this all sorted out..." The hard carved face was sheepish. If his feet hadn't been so big and his boots so heavy, he would have scuffed them in the dirt.

"You want to know."

"Well, yeah. We're friends. Friends know what's going on in friends' lives. Particularly when it hurts so much."

"I'm not hurt, Tiny," Mac said into an abrupt hush as an engine sputtered and died. "Not anymore."

"No?"

"No."

"Have it your way, Mac, but if you need me, I'm here."

"I know." Mac grinned at the great hulk of a man. Tiny, with a heart as soft as his body was hard, clumsy on the ground, an angel climbing steel. Resuming his walk, he called over his shoulder. "If I need you, Tiny, I'll call."

The hospital corridor was as antiseptic in its hush as in its cleanliness. Sound wasn't absent as much as contained. Even the laughter was muted, low-key, but reminded there is always hope.

Mac shrugged out of his parka, tossing it on the first chair in the first waiting room he passed. His step thudded solidly over the polished floor. He was tempted to tiptoe, but abandoned the thought. Tiptoeing wouldn't help, and he would look silly in the process. A rhino in rough dress mincing to a tea party. Big, ugly and ungainly.

He was smiling at the comparison when he pushed his way through the double doors of the canteen. And suddenly there he was, the rhino at the party.

The room was filled with women and men clustered at small tables. Nurses, doctors, parents of ailing children. Some dressed in white, others in bright colors. They were neat, combed, controlled. Not one was dark and brawny, with crow's feet and callused hands. No jeans or heavy shirts, or boots laced to the ankle.

To the woman who observed from a corner table, none was as commanding, making the space his as naturally as breathing, dominating with his aura of raw, animal magnetism. None as handsome, with sun streaks blending into silver that threaded through his rich brown hair. None turned her knees to water and her throat to desert.

He wasn't a tall man, or a heavy one, but he seemed too big for the room. Too alive. Too vital. Too much. A bonfire in the dark? A tsunami in a woodland pool? A wolf among doves?

Jennifer watched and waited, seeing how he gripped the half-open door, scanning the room. How he moved aside with the gallantry she'd loved, letting two very young nurses pass him by, their quick looks of awe lost on him.

Then his searching gaze found her, and for Jennifer there were no others in the canteen. Only Mac, weaving his way through tables, and she, waiting, wondering why he'd come.

Slowly, as she regathered her wits, she saw heads turn discreetly and gazes flicker away. She heard the murmur of conversation that had dwindled at his entrance begin again. She saw distracted speakers and unheeding listeners feign no interest in the stranger who walked among them.

Mac was as focused and as intense as he'd been at Georgia Tech. She would've laughed at the familiarness of the ingrained trait, but laughter was beyond her when she was the purpose of that intensity. Her gaze was fixed on him as he passed through the room, unaware he gathered an audience as a wave gathers sand.

A tsunami? She searched for the right analogy but had no time for another as he stopped at her table. Beads of water glinted in his hair. His shirt was faded denim. Sleeves turned back over burly arms, buttons strained over his chest. Feet planted, fists at his hips, he was overpoweringly masculine.

Yes, she decided, a tsunami, and today the canteen was his woodland pool. She forced a smile. "Good morning."

Mac inclined his head in response, but didn't return her smile. "How are you?"

"Perfectly recovered, thanks to you." Then, because he was formidable towering over her and because he wouldn't sit until invited, she indicated a chair. "I only have a few more minutes, but would you care to join me?"

Inclining his head again, he reversed a chair. Sitting astride it with his arms resting on the back, he judged her recovery for himself. Today her skirt was navy, the blouse a paler shade of blue, the scarf stripes of both with varying shades of purple. She was very proper, with her proper decorum, in her proper dress.

The enchanting hoyden had become a woman, her youthful exuberance replaced by flawless dignity. He wondered if her patients ever smeared little handprints on her clothing or tugged the scarf from her hair, rumpling that dignity, touching her as he wanted to.

He'd been inordinately pleased when in her distress she wanted no lover called to comfort her. He hadn't examined why. Now it was impossible to believe there was no one, that the cool, untouched quality did not draw men to her in droves, daring them, driving them to distraction. She was quiet, but not quiescent. Banked fires of passion lay barely beneath the surface. What unattached male could resist the challenge of stirring its embers, risking its burn?

It was disturbing that he cared whether there might be men in her life. This possessiveness was not what he expected when he approached her. But with an honesty as innate as his tenacity, Mac admitted an irrational jealousy he had no right to harbor.

He'd spent ten years in another world. Long years of grueling labor. Years of trying to put her out of his mind. He'd come home to stay at last, sure that he could put his life in order. And a single encounter proved that ten years had not been enough.

He had unfinished business with the woman Jennifer had become. The woman who was his wife.

He didn't understand Jennifer or himself, but he would. He turned his incredible concentration on her, considering her unnatural control, the rigidness of it. The perfect stillness. A lingering effect of the migraine? Was every totally calculated move dictated by the heightened awareness she'd described? The ghost of her pain haunting her at every ill-advised move?

His penetrating study told him no. Her eyes were clear, her gaze steady. The vein at her temple, dark and pulsing when the agony was upon her, was only a faint ribbon of blue. Her hands hadn't once strayed to the scarf that held her hair captive. She had spoken the truth. No flashing lights and piercing pain lurked at the edge of her vision. If she was pale beneath the minimal makeup, it could be attributed to the unforgiving glare of fluorescence, the pallor of winter. Or the strain of his unexpected appearance? Her next words had him discarding the latter.

"I was hoping to see you." A calm voice, this time without the rasp of battle.

"Were you?" He did a second, instinctive sweep of her body, this one pure appreciation. Tiny was right. She was, in his phrase, for damn sure a fine-looking woman.

"Yes." Jennifer resisted the urge to move beneath his appraisal.

"Why?"

Had he always been this reticent? The dour Scot to the hilt? Jennifer laced her fingers one over the other to ensure that she didn't tap, or fidget, or bite a nail. "To thank you."

"Now you have."

"Yes."

"If I hadn't come, what would you have done?"

The question surprised her. "Gone to the site, of course."

"Of course." Exactly what he would've expected. The perfect diction, perfect dress, perfect protocol. A personal expression of gratitude for a personal service. Not bending an inch from propriety. And again that aloofness that translated in a man's mind into seething sexuality barely held in check. He wondered if she dreamed that the more distant she became, the more precise, the more any red-blooded man wanted to see her hair flying wild and free in a tangle about her shoulders, with the prim little buttons of her prim little blouse lying on the floor.

She would be magnificent with the swell of her full breasts rising over a lacy, dainty scrap of a bra. A perfect globe to fill his hand. When he suckled, the nipple would be hard beneath the gauzy, delicate pattern of the lace.

A schoolboy fantasy, so real it left him hollow and aching. Mac smiled at his foolishness. A genuine smile that changed his features, softening them, offering a glimpse of the youth who had become the man.

Jennifer froze at his silence and at the smile. He was keeping her off-balance, playing the stern Highlander one minute, the charming tease the next. It was difficult to keep her promise to herself that she would be indifferent and remote. An image impossible to maintain when she had no idea what she'd done to prompt the smile and the glimmer of mischief.

Mac rested his chin on his folded arms, his eyes narrowed, visualizing sultry lace beneath the sexless clothes. His smile widened. The mischief became more than a glimmer.

Jennifer couldn't stand not knowing. She grew frustrated, forgot not to be nervous or dignified. Her laced fingers flew apart in an impatient gesture. There was irritation in her tone. "What?"

Mac laughed, sending shivers of memory down her spine. "I was imagining how cute you would look in a hard hat."

"Oh." Jennifer was disconcerted. From the lazy, sensual look in his eyes, she hadn't expected something so innocent.

"I'm not sure we have one small enough." Mac continued the lie as a matter of fact, as if a blush had not crept from the slope of her breasts to her throat. "I'll order one, just in case you might want to visit the site at a later date."

"No," she said quickly, uncomfortable with her own thoughts. "That isn't necessary. I won't be visiting the site."

"What? Not interested in the latest edition to your workplace? Surely Daddy has a couple of million or so invested."

Jennifer's hands were tightly under control again. She only shook her head in response to his sarcasm.

"No, you aren't interested? Or no, Daddy hasn't a few million invested?"

"Of course I'm interested, but I can see what I need to from my office." Her fingers began writhing about each other. "And, no, my father has nothing invested here."

Something in her tone disturbed him, something he couldn't quite isolate. It had to do with her father, the man who had controlled her life by giving her the world. Mac backed away. He hadn't intended to drag out old histories in a hospital canteen.

"Mac, why did you come here today?"

"Not to fight with you."

"Then why?"

"To judge for myself how you are."

"I see." She didn't really believe him, but if that was how he wanted it, she was willing to leave it and be grateful to slide by so easily. Picking up a carton, she realized the chilled juice was gone and set it back down again. The empty box was her excuse to escape. "Now that you know I survived, I'll leave you to get on with your day." She crumpled a napkin and took up the juice carton. "Break's over."

"Jenn—"

"If you have time, I recommend the juice bar. It's fresh and cold." Her voice overrode his deliberately. She didn't want to hear anything else he had to say. Pushing back her seat, she stood, not looking at him, not offering her hand. "Goodbye, Mac. I don't suppose there's any need for us to see each other again."

"Have dinner with me."

The carton crushed in her grasp. He'd caught her off guard again. "What?"

Patiently, as to a willfully unheeding child, "I asked you to have dinner with me."

She moved her head wonderingly, trying to clear her thoughts. "Why on earth should we have dinner together?"

Mac stood, the training of a lifetime asserting itself. Never sit when a woman stands. Dare—brother, father figure, friend—had been adamant. A natural gallantry. "For more reasons than either of us can count. Because there are unfinished affairs and secrets between us."

"Secrets!" The debris gathered from the table spilled from her fingers, as the guttural word tumbled from lips rimmed in white. "What secrets?"

"I thought you would tell me." With studied nonchalance he gathered up her crumpled napkin and the carton with a trickle of ruby red spilling from it. "About what prompted your profession. The trouble with your father."

"There is no trouble with my father."

"You haven't quarreled?"

"Not in nine years." She was icy now. The snow maiden who could freeze with a look.

"My mistake." But was it? He'd taken a shot in the dark, and God only knew what target he'd hit. He hadn't expected her reaction.

"Your mistake, indeed." She twisted her wrist to glance at her watch. "Show's over. People have stared at us long enough, and I should be on duty."

He followed her from the canteen, her garbage tossed into the nearest refuse container as they marched like martinets down the hall to a stairway. She stormed the risers at a half jog, then stalked another hall at a brisk pace. Mac kept abreast, taking two steps to three of hers. When she passed through a door marked private, he went there, too.

A secretary looked up from a computer, her ready smile dying at the sight of a brawny roughneck following the diminutive doctor. Jennifer murmured a terse greeting, something about midmorning appointments, and hurried on.

"Hold the appointments," Mac instructed the grim-faced woman.

"I beg your pardon?" A conditioned response. This particular secretary had never begged anything in her life.

"Ten minutes." Mac held up both hands, fingers splayed. "Count 'em. Ten."

Sally, with her hair cut so short she could pass for a storm trooper, decided to act the part. With ill-concealed relish she spun her chair into the fray. "Just who do you think you are, coming in here giving orders?"

"An abject request, not an order."

Her wintry eyes did not waver.

"And I don't think, Ms.—" Mac's gaze flickered to the name plate on her desk and back again to her face "—Ms. Brown, I *know* who I am."

Sally Brown cast a contemptuous look at his dusty boots, the faded jeans and frayed shirt, ignoring completely that he wore them better than other men wore designer styles and labels. What she didn't ignore was that this handsome ruffian was harassing her boss.

It happened. Sometimes an agitated father resenting that the doctor had no miracle for his child. Sometimes a mother too distraught to understand the cruelty of her harangue. Some persisted, as this man had, bringing their grievance from the hospital floor to the office. But never for long, not as long as Sally Brown lived.

She had not risen from her chair. At six-three in stocking feet and with the build of a linebacker, her body was her last line of intimidation. In those rare, stubborn cases, all she ever had to do was stand, towering and glowering, and the problem invariably resolved itself.

This one might require the full treatment, she thought, but not yet. In a voice thick with frost she suggested, "Since you know so well who you are, why don't you tell *me* just who that might be."

Mac leaned on her desk, his weight on his knuckles, his eyes level with hers. "I'm her husband, Ms. Brown. If you want to get cute about it, call me Mr. McLachlan." He didn't blink, didn't move, then softly, "Any more questions, Ms. Brown?"

Sally opened her mouth and gulped air.

"Then I can expect you to give us the time?" At her nod the steel left his voice. "Thank you, Ms. Brown."

Mac straightened from the desk. If she'd stood he would've been several inches shorter than she, but as intimidating. Until he smiled. Then Sally Brown wondered why she'd ever thought he was a ruffian.

"Ten minutes?"

This one could charm birds from trees. "Yes, sir."

"Good. That should give both of us enough time."

"Both of us?" The big woman with the brush cut was puzzled now.

"Certainly. Ten minutes for me to make my pitch to the doc. Ten for you to make a call or two with the latest gossip, resolving the mystery of who I am."

"I wouldn't!"

"Sure you would, Sally." Mac's drawling laugh was congenial, including her in a conspiracy. "I've given you an exclusive. Make the most of it."

Mac backed away with one last glance. Coupled with his blunt declaration of his identity and the congenial about-face, it was enough to send Sally back to her computer, head down, eyes glued to the screen, hand itching for the telephone.

A dozen steps and he caught up with Jennifer at a door with a brass sign designating it as her private office. She was standing like a stone image, staring at him, her mouth open from her gasp of shock, her knuckles white as she clung to the knob.

When he brushed her hand aside and opened the door, she stepped through, barely giving him time to close it behind him before she rounded on him. "Why did you do that? Why on earth did you say you're my husband?"

"I am your husband, Jennifer."

"Only because of a legal procedure left undone." Arms folded over her breasts, holding herself intact, she was pacing as he'd paced through the weekend.

"The lady asked." Mac shrugged. "I told her."

Jennifer stopped by a wall of books. Books of a profession that offered serenity for the troubled, but there was no serenity in her. "You told her all right! Then you practically insisted that she tell the entire hospital."

"What harm will it do?" He advanced into the room that was as simple and as functional as her home. "Better they know the truth than to speculate heaven knows what."

"Speculate?" There was a blankness tempering her anger. She had no idea what he meant.

"I can see you aren't privy to the gossip mill. We've been its topic for weeks."

"We?"

"We. You. Me. And the assumption there's more between us than meets the eye."

"That's ridiculous!" she exclaimed sharply. "Before the weekend I didn't know you were in the country, and certainly not that you were here."

"I know." He would've been surprised if she had *known* of everyone's noting the correlation of their names, their ages, their marriages. The delicious hope that he was the mystery husband returned from exotic places, coupled with tales of either hero or villain, depending on the version, performing secret deeds. She worked far too hard to have time for down and dirty gossip sessions with the staff.

"How can you be so sure I didn't know?" Her tone was cutting. Not caring that she reversed herself, she was ready to quarrel on any issue.

"Your surprise when you saw me was genuine. And I suspect if you'd known I was here before then, you would have run."

She had begun to pace again. Her back was turned, but now she swung around. "I don't run, Mac." Every word was precise, clipped. "Not anymore."

"All right." He'd surprised himself with that—the idea had come from nowhere. In retrospect he saw it was slightly skewed. She wouldn't run, at least not physically. "A better choice of words would be, you would have avoided me more scrupulously."

She didn't deny this. "Better if you'd done the same."

"No, Jennifer, we have problems to resolve. We might as well begin by facing them and by being honest."

"You face them. You resolve them. Since you've been so honest with Sally about matters that are no concern of hers, I'd say you've made a good start."

She was in a towering rage. Her teeth were clamped together, her eyes blazing, her breath coming in short-hard pants. Mac knew she was thinner, but now that every angry rise of her chest threatened the buttons of her blouse, he saw not exactly thinner everywhere. The girlish slenderness had transformed into narrow-hipped, full-bodied shapeliness. She was an intelligent, interesting woman, and more beautiful in her anger than she'd ever been. "Have dinner with me."

"What!" She stopped in mid-tirade, glaring at him.

The same question. The same answer for her stubborn resistance. "I said, have dinner with me."

"As simple as that, after that little fiasco with Sally?" She paced again, this time to her desk.

"Yes, as simple as that."

He was relentless, a broken record. "Absolutely not."

"Is it Rick?" Another shot in the dark.

"Rick? Rick Casson, from Tech?" Jennifer was genuinely astonished. "Why would you think he has anything to do with anything?"

"You mentioned that you'd talked with him about South America and my work there. Since he's divorced, it's possible."

"Rick and Karen are divorced?"

"You didn't know?" He suppressed his own surprise.

"How could I? The only time I've seen either of them since graduation was years ago. They were together then."

"Is there someone else?"

"That's none of your business."

"It's always a husband's business if his wife has another man in her life."

Jennifer sat heavily in her chair, her hands framing her head. For a long moment she sat, her fingers massaging the soft flesh above her brows.

Mac was instantly concerned. "Another headache?"

"Yes." Her hands went to the arms of her chair, gripping them. "One that walks and talks. I have patients to see, Mac. I'm sure you can find your way back to the site."

"Then you won't have dinner with me?"

"Not tonight. Not ever."

"Give me one good reason." He hooked his hands in the back pockets of his jeans. A move that accentuated the breadth of his shoulders.

"Because it would serve no purpose. Because we have nothing to discuss beyond a divorce, and that needn't be done over dinner."

"And if I don't agree?"

Jennifer rested her hands, palms down, in the exact center of her desk. Control through order. "You asked for a reason. I gave you two. Now, as I said, I have work to do."

He moved to the side of her desk, trailing a knuckle over the curved edge. He was so close he could have touched her. All he needed was to lift his hands from smooth, burnished cherry. He didn't lift his hands. He didn't touch her. Almost casually he asked, "What are you afraid of, Jennifer?"

"Afraid?" Her heart was a trip-hammer threatening to explode from its violent pulsing. She dared not look away from him. Dared not let him see what his question had done to her. With an effort that took every ounce of her strength, she took up a sheaf of reports, shuffling them, disrupting their sequence. "I'm not afraid of anything, Mac. Now, if you would go, please, I do have a lot to do."

"I can see you do." He glanced at the reports, and at the list of appointments that would take her through the afternoon and into the evening. "I'm going, but only for now."

Jennifer didn't respond. Clinging to an outward calm, she sat as she was as he strode to the door. When he stopped, his eyes meeting hers, she didn't look away.

"Make no mistake about it, Jennifer. There's unfinished business between us, and I'll be back to resolve it."

"There's nothing to resolve. After you left, my life was havoc and disorder. Peace was a long time coming, but I have it now, and I don't want to lose it." Her hand shook, papers crackled. "What do you want, Mac? Why are you here?"

"What do I want? The same things you want. Order. Peace. Why am I here?" He opened the door, the brighter light from the waiting room turning him to a somber figure. "Perhaps when I know why you're here and why your peace is so fragile, I'll have the answer to that."

When he was gone Jennifer sat, holding the reports, staring at the door where he'd stood. She had no idea how much time passed before she laid the yellow, sweat-soaked papers on her desk, trying with no success to smooth out the damaging creases. In defeat she left her desk, moving to the window. If anyone had asked, she would have insisted she wasn't thinking about Mac. Yet of their own volition her eyes turned to squares of steel that only vaguely resembled a building. And finally to the path beaten between the site and the hospital.

He was there, wearing the familiar parka, walking with the confidence of a man who knew what he wanted and would have it.

"And what is that?" The question was a hollow one, and she had no more answers for herself than she had for Mac. "Dear heaven," she whispered, "what do you want?"

For longer than she knew she watched him, her mind empty of everything but her memories. A giant of a man met him, flung an arm about his shoulders and walked with him. She was still watching when they moved beyond her vision.

An awestruck Sally announced her next appointment, and Jennifer was again the dedicated Dr. McLachlan.

Four

Jennifer drank in the night air. Cool, biting, with no cloying reminders of medicine. The trail she walked adjoined a path from her back terrace. The trail led to a community park, a neat square with groomed, meandering paths and meticulously unstructured flower beds. There would be pansies soon, and hyacinths.

Then daffodils.

Through spring and summer, and into autumn there would be flowers. Each in its perfect niche, a perfect blend, as if nature planned it. The many hands of the Gentlemen's Garden Club of Barclay were never intrusive.

The park was nature coaxed, at times directed, but never tamed. A joint effort, a work of art, lovelier than man or nature could make it alone. It was Jennifer's favorite place, the reason for buying her brick-and-wood house.

The peace within its shadowy borders lured her, healed her. After a long day and a lonely dinner, it had become increasingly natural to wander across her terrace, through her own unskilled efforts at gardening, to these brick-lined pathways. Steeped in its artless harmony, she found her own. From its serenity, she drew the strength to do each day what she must.

The park was her magic elixir. Her prescription for the needs of heart and mind. Tonight she wandered its paths seeking that elixir. There were no flowers now, and only the moon and half-hidden ground lamps lighted her way. But there were evergreens and ivy and the scent of fallen pine needles crushed beneath her step. And the light was enough.

The way she'd chosen looped in an lazy pattern with no destination apparent. Abruptly, to the uninitiated, shrubs and trees gave way to small commons. This destination of converging routes was Jennifer's destination, as well.

Passing clay courts abandoned hours ago by even the most dedicated tennis devotee, she moved to the playground. Empty seesaws creaked, and drooping swings clattered their chains.

Ghost children, Jennifer pretended, stealing this quiet time for themselves. With the moon for their sun and the wind as their voice, the children in her mind found joy the real world denied them. Climbing onto a low corded wall, with her legs crossed at the ankles, she closed her eyes to listen to their play.

In her waking dream there was always laughter and skipping footsteps. Always joy, and skills such as hers went unneeded. A dream, only a dream, one that offered respite. When the troubles of her practice became too great, she brought them here. For a time, the burdens would be lifted. Tonight the utopia escaped her.

Far above, treetops rustled in a high-flying wind. A leaf driven by the breeze below skittered over the clay courts with the sound of a fingernail drawn against a blackboard. A discarded tube that had once held tennis balls tumbled from a bench, rolling with an uneven rhythm across a graveled walk.

Normal sounds. On another night she wouldn't have noticed them. Tonight they reminded her too strongly of the real world. And before it could ever be, the dream was shattered.

Jennifer stirred and opened her eyes, her frail hold on the peace of the park gone. The troubles she'd brought to the commons would not be still.

Mac.

For a week she'd managed to avoid him, but he was always in her mind. The time was coming when she must deal with him. In ten years a strong man had become stronger, a child matured into a woman, and lovers were only strangers. Yet he disturbed her, more than any stranger should.

When he was near her heart ached, but not from unrequited love. Mac was a bittersweet memory. A love that would never come again. She believed and accepted that it could be no other way for either of them. Yet there were other memories his probing awakened. Memories more bitter than sweet, that held the answers he was seeking.

She was afraid. Afraid that his quest for answers too devastating to face would tear her life asunder. Jennifer shivered. Could she survive destruction a second time?

She was stronger now, she had to believe strong enough, and hiding in the dark resolved nothing.

Reluctantly she got to her feet. A drifting cloud covered the moon, and only the light of the lamps was left. She had no concept of how long she'd wandered the trails or sat in the commons, only that the hour was late. As she turned for home, she realized the park had failed her. Sadly she wondered if its peace would ever come again.

Head bowed, she climbed the hillock retracing the wooded path she'd taken. Cold she hadn't noticed before numbed her feet and legs and made her clumsy. A loose stone rolled beneath her unsteady step. She would have fallen if not for hard, powerful hands clamping her shoulders.

The park was her haven. Nothing bad had ever happened within its boundaries and she'd never been afraid. Yet her first response was fear, her instinct to fight. With a silent cry and claws unsheathed, she struggled against the forceful grasp.

"Jennifer."

Intent on turning to fight, she didn't understand. Not even when arms like granite embraced her, drawing her backward against an unyielding body.

"Jennifer! Don't!" Lips brushed against her ear, hot breath burned across her cheek. The arms that held her prisoner only tightened when her nails raked across the thin flesh of his hand. "Don't be afraid."

The voice was persuasive, its familiarity piercing her frenzy. "Mac? Oh, God! Mac." She slumped against him, not caring that he saw the weakness in her relief, or that his arms supported her. "I thought..."

"Shh," he murmured against her hair. "I know what you thought. I'm the one who didn't think. You were falling and might've been hurt, I simply reacted." Turning her toward him, he looked down at her. In the dark of the moon he could see little. "Are you all right?"

"I will be." She tried to move back, her step wobbling.

"Easy." Mac gathered her back against him, his hand stroking her bound hair. "Give it a minute."

Until his warmth surrounded her she hadn't known how cold she'd become. Or how quiet the night, until the steady rhythm of his heart pounded beneath her ear. With the aftermath of fear sapping her strength, she was tempted to sink into that warmth and let his strength be her own. But she'd been her own source of strength too long to tolerate even this little dependence.

Palms flat against his chest, she pushed away. He was reluctant to let her go, but did not keep her. Still touching him, her face lifted, she saw only the dark shape of his head, the broad body. "You've made a habit of coming out of the dark when I need you. I should thank you."

"And I should apologize. I did more harm than good."

"I didn't die from fear, and I don't have a broken and bloody knee, either, so let's call it an incident that worked out for the best."

"Next time, I'll look before I leap." He offered his left hand for her inspection. "Tangling with you can be dangerous."

Even in the darkness, the price he'd paid for his gallantry was visible. His hand was ghostly in the night, but scratches crossing from wrist to fingertips were stark with black welling blood. The wounds were not serious, but he was a man who worked with his hands, and Mac was left-handed. Tomorrow the wounds would be very sore. And there was always the chance of infection.

She heard herself saying, "Come with me. I'll attend to that."

"It's nothing." He tucked the hand behind him. "I've had worse."

"Maybe you have." Jennifer didn't relent. "But I wasn't responsible."

"You'd worry if I didn't let you offer me tea and sympathy?"

"Iodine and a bandage."

"Iodine?" He grimaced, anticipating the sting.

"Sorry."

"Are you, Jennifer?"

"For the scratches, not the iodine."

He watched the play of broken light on her face. "You're a tough one, aren't you?" Then thoughtfully, "A fighter."

"I learned to be." With his face in shadow he had the advantage, but she gave nothing away with her expression or her tone. "I had to."

Blunt statements that left more unsaid than said. Pursuing them in the park was as unsuitable as the hospital parking lot. He'd been too abrupt, too insistent before. A stranger, coming out of the past, prying into her life. He wouldn't make that mistake again.

She needed time. He knew now he did, as well. Time to know each other, to understand the people they'd become, before delving into what had been.

"A tough lady." He stroked her cheek, his right hand gentle against her cool flesh. "Too tough to offer a drop of tea to a wayfarer on a chilly night?"

"Tea?" Jennifer didn't flinch away from his touch, nor did her gaze waver. "Or sympathy?"

Mac chuckled. "Which choice should I make?"

"Take the tea," she shot back. Drawing his injured hand from his back and a handkerchief from her pocket, she wound it once around his palm and tied it tightly. Ignoring the sudden clench of his fingers, she patted the bandage. "Tea would be warmer."

"My thoughts exactly." Looping a casual arm around her shoulders, pleased that she did not grow rigid with the contact, he walked with her to the trail. The moon chose that moment to glide from the clouds. By the time it fully divested itself of its misty veil, they were deep in the evergreen forest.

"Have a seat at the table, and I'll be back before you know it." Jennifer tossed her jacket and his onto a chair and hurried down the hall.

Mac examined the room again, looking for clues that would explain her. And again, there was only the surface simplicity offering comfort to its guests, but nothing of Jennifer. Beyond the stamp of her style, she'd deliberately excluded anything of herself. There were no photographs, no credentials or reminders of accomplishment. No mementos of the past. No evidence of her father.

If he could believe what he saw, she had set herself adrift from all she'd known. The only visible sentiment lay in the creations made by her patients.

Mac let his gaze stray to a collection of misshapen baskets and clay figures. Plaster of paris disks with tiny handprints preserved in them. Collages of jagged magazine clippings. The singular drawing in its place of honor. These were her treasures. Her past, her present.

Once he'd thought her home was a reflection of need for order after the chaos of her work. Now he was certain it was her work that brought order, and the chaos had been her life. Something had nearly destroyed her. Something so terrible she couldn't bear any reminders. Despair rose in him as he wondered if he'd done this to her.

"This should serve." Basin in hand, Jennifer slipped into the seat by his side. The sleeves of her shirt had been rolled back. She was a woman prepared to work.

His face was grim when he faced her. "Jennifer, I'm sorry." His voice was raw and haunted from his thoughts. "This isn't necessary."

"I think it is." She brushed his protest aside and, taking his hand in hers, began to remove her handkerchief.

"It's late. I can see to this myself."

"Actually it's early." She hadn't looked at him, all her concentration on her task. "And I'll see to it."

Mac looked down at her hands. Her fingers were strong, the nails short and unvarnished. Competent hands. "Call one o'clock in the morning early or late, it makes for a long day. You must be tired."

"An inherent trait among the staff at Barclay." She was unperturbed by his familiarity with her schedule. Without ceremony she immersed his hand in the steaming solution in the basin. Patting his shoulder in her best physician's manner, she stood. "Let that soak while I put on the kettle."

"Good Lord! What is this?" It took every ounce of determination to keep his hand in the solution.

"A disinfectant." The kettle was filled. The burner beneath it a red eye.

"Will it leave the skin?"

She slid her hands into the back pockets of her jeans and leaned against the counter. One sneaker-clad foot propped over the other, she was more relaxed than she'd been with him previously. A look that was nearly a grin danced over her face. "I made it a little strong. Infection, you know."

"One question."

"Only one? What a change."

"If I need this to disinfect scratches you made, I have to wonder if you've had your rabies vaccine."

Jennifer laughed. Her head was thrown back, her hair streamed from the scarf that held it and over her shoulder. "Not lately, but perhaps I should."

The kettle began to steam, and for a while she devoted her attention to the making of tea. When it was set to brew she crossed to the table with a towel. Taking his hand from the water, she blotted it dry. Her touch as gentle as the soaking had been caustic, she applied ointment, a square of gauze and adhesive.

"You do that very well," he observed thoughtfully.

"Part of my training." She dismissed her skill as easily as she had her long hours at work.

"Before you chose to specialize in healing hearts and minds, rather than bodies?"

"A long time before."

Mac fell silent, content to watch her work.

She was winding a length of gauze around his hand and securing it with tape when she looked up to find him watching her intently. With his hand still in hers she returned his look. His eyes were still the impossible blue, too dark to be believed. A family trait, he'd told her once, but somehow she thought they would've changed, faded in the tropical sun, or lost their glitter. Instead, they were the same marvelous eyes that had smiled at her in a tavern so long ago.

Realizing she was staring, she was the first to look away. "I, ah, I think that should be sufficient." Releasing his hand, she scrubbed her palms on the legs of her jeans, but the remembrance of his touch couldn't be scrubbed away.

"No iodine?" His words were lazy, teasing, his tone soft.

"The soaking should've done as well." Jennifer pushed back her chair with no idea where she was going. When she was on her feet she remembered the tea.

"Jennifer." Mac caught her fingers in his own, the deep blue of his gaze holding her as strongly as his grasp.

She wanted to stay there with the quiet surrounding them. She wanted to run. In the end she did neither. With a quizzical lift of her brows she murmured, "Yes, Mac?"

He shook his head, at a sudden loss for words. Then he shrugged, shoulders tugging the seams of his shirt. "Nothing. Just thank you."

With a wordless sound she drew her hand away. "Try to keep the bandage clean or change it often."

"I'll come by your office for you to dress it."

"That won't be necessary. I'll send supplies with you."

Mac regarded the expert bandaging. Flexing his fingers, he folded the injured hand into a fist and rested it on the table. With his eyes fixed on the slash of white across his tanned skin he muttered, "So we're back to it?"

"I beg your pardon? Back to what?"

His gaze settled again on her. "For a little while tonight you unbent a bit. Now you're back to avoiding me."

"You're mistaken. I'm not avoiding you." To underscore her point she gathered a tray from a cabinet, arranging the teapot, cups and napkins on it. When she returned to her seat he was still watching. Careful not to let her hand shake, she filled a cup and handed it to him.

Mac took it, but did not drink. He might've been reading tea leaves if there'd been any. "You remember."

Her cup halfway to her lips, she paused, a question in her look.

"You remember I take my tea as it comes from the pot."

Jennifer set her untouched tea aside. "It isn't an important thing to remember."

"I know."

He drank then from his cup, and Jennifer was left with the thought that he attached greater satisfaction to the remembrance of small details than to large. The simplicity of his statement, its significance, sent an unsettling tremor through her. Determined she wouldn't lose control of this strange interlude, she changed the subject abruptly. "Why were you in the park tonight?"

She'd intended to catch him off guard, but his answer made no effort to evade or hedge. "I was waiting for you."

Barely containing her surprise at the straightforward admission, she leaned back in her chair, her eyes narrowed, one finger tapping the rim of her cup. "Why would you wait for me? How did you know I would be in the park?"

"Today was a particularly rough day. You walk off the tensions and the restlessness of rough days in the park."

"*I* know today was a rough day. *I* know I walk in the park. You haven't told me how *you* know."

"Your secretary." He looked from her level gaze to her tapping finger and back again. "She knows, and she worries. When she worries she talks."

Jennifer pushed back her chair and stood, more surprised than angry. "You've been gossiping with my secretary?"

"Not exactly. Actually, I'm the last person your private watchdog would talk with. She isn't sure yet if she trusts me. I suspect she thinks my being here will hurt you." He watched as she moved to a counter, saw her lift her face to the drawing by the window. "Is that what you think, Jennifer?"

She turned back to him. "What?" Then before he could rephrase his question she shook her head. "No, of course not. It never occurred to me you intend to hurt me."

"Intend?" He was utterly still. Only the slow rise of a controlling breath revealed his quickened interest. "An odd choice of words. I can't help but wonder if it implies that inadvertently my reappearance in your life is painful."

Her arms were folded over her breasts. Her hands moved restlessly from shoulder to elbow and back again. She still wore no jewelry other than a small watch. Her fingers were bare. "That would be ridiculous, wouldn't it? Time is a great healer. Even memories fade.

"We were wrong for each other from the first, Mac. You knew it, but I was too young and too spoiled to understand. Our marriage was headed for disaster. Perhaps it could have been salvaged, perhaps not. None of that matters now. You made a choice, I made mine, and our lives took separate paths. We couldn't go back even if we wanted to. That foolish young girl doesn't exist anymore. She grew up a long time ago."

"But too late for us."

"Yes," she said softly. "Too late for us."

"Would it surprise you that I've done some growing up myself? That I can admit now that a part of the failure of our marriage was mine? I married a person from another world and in my presumption demanded she conform completely to mine."

"There was never room for compromise for either of us, was there?"

Mac scowled and slid the cooling tea aside. For an arrogant man, admitting his own arrogance wasn't easy. "The McLachlans aren't known for compromise."

Jennifer almost smiled then, remembering an applicable anecdote he'd told her years before. "A family of tubby sots, as your nephew called it?"

"Tyler was only a babe then, and he was speaking of Dare, but he had us pegged. We are a family of stubborn Scots."

"I was immature and pampered. You were stubborn and arrogant. A formula for disaster. But it's over, and all that's left is an empty marriage. Now that you're back in the country to stay, you'll be wanting a divorce so you can get on with that part of your life." From out of nowhere she felt a burgeoning sorrow, and wondered why the official severing of a marriage that hadn't been a marriage in a decade should hurt. Was it that facing one's own shortcomings, even after so long a time, was not easy?

Mac saw a somber expression flicker over her face, and with it the drawn look of fatigue. "I didn't mean to get into this, Jennifer. I didn't deliberately waylay you in the park to create an opportunity to bring it up."

"Then why did you come?" Her hands no longer moved over her arms. Instead, as tension spiraled, her fingers clutched at the sleeves of her blouse, threatening the fabric. Sheer willpower kept her on her feet.

Leaving his seat, Mac went to her, to lend his strength to hers. Taking her by the shoulders, he held her. "I'd heard of your taxing day and of your walks in the park and that Sally was concerned. I came to see for myself that you weren't in danger."

"My secretary has shown a surprising lack of discretion in discussing my habits. But if it puts your mind at ease, Sally is overreacting. I'm not a fool, I don't court danger. The park is patrolled, and security knows I walk there."

"And if I'd been an assailant, where was your security?"

"You weren't an assailant."

Mac was not so easily appeased. He shook her gently. "But if I had been?"

Jennifer glanced down at the bandage that shone like new snow against the dark emerald of her blouse. Her full lips compressed into a grim line. "Then I would have fought you."

"Just like that, you would've fought?"

"Just like that."

She was small. At the moment she was fragile, but he could see that even now she would be a formidable opponent. The slow, insistent throb in his hand left little doubt of it. But he was twice her size. However much she fought him, no matter how formidable, she couldn't have won.

A look into the shadowed brown of her eyes told him Jennifer knew. But still would have fought to the last breath. She was that kind of a woman now. A hell of a woman. And she was his wife. "Jennifer—"

"No." With her hand she held him away. "No more. You said you didn't intend to get into this, and you're right, we shouldn't. Not now. Not anytime. My safety, and what I do with my time and why, is my concern. Your only consideration is the service you've agreed to perform for the hospital. Our meeting was coincidence. When your work is done, there will be nothing to hold you here. Just as there was nothing to hold you in a marriage that should never have happened. Get your divorce, Mac, and forget me. Don't waste your time wondering who I am now, and why. Just forget me."

"As you've forgotten me?"

"Yes."

"Little liar." She smelled of fresh air and a subtle perfume. Together they pulsed about him, stirred him. He could hear the perfume-laden breath drawn into his lungs, feel the strong steady beat of his heart. He was falling beneath the spell of her gorgeous eyes, drowning in pale amber dappled with gold like the sun. He touched her cheek again, the bandages soft against the prominent curve.

Nothing changed at his touch. Not even the flutter of a lash or a frown. Yet there was something in the depths of her sun-swept eyes, and he knew he was right. His hand cradled the curve of her jaw, keeping her only by sheer contact. "You remember," he murmured, savoring her scent. "You remember everything."

Jennifer moved her head one slow half turn. An almost imperceptible denial that brought her lips in brushing contact with the heel of his hand. A current of electricity couldn't have been more shocking than the innocent touch. She was reeling from the exquisite heat that danced barely beneath the surface of her very proper decorum. It was that heat that turned her voice hoarse and lent a razor's edge to her strangled cry. "No."

"Yes." His rebuttal was low, suggestive. He dipped his head to hers, stopping only inches from her mouth. His words were guileless, his husky tone was not. "You remember I take my tea straight, that I'm left-handed. That I'm stubborn and arrogant, a McLachlan through and through." He traced a lazy trail to her lips, the slow, tender pressure tugging at her mouth. "I'd gamble you remember my fraternal twin's dimple is here." His nail scratched lightly at the corner of her mouth. "While mine is..."

"A good bit farther south," Jennifer said, drawing on every bit of restraint to keep from slapping his hand away.

Mac chuckled, a delighted sound. "So you do remember."

"Don't flatter yourself, McLachlan. Any girl would remember that about *any* man, if he was her first."

Mac wasn't to be bested. "Ah, yes. There is that. You were always a source of surprise. Never what I expected. Life with you would never have been boring." He chuckled again. "It's nearly two in the morning, and we're both dead on our feet. I don't know who the hell you are anymore or why I should care, but here you are with those glorious golden eyes glaring at me, and I'm as surprised and intrigued as I was ten years ago."

"Don't be." She couldn't keep herself from moving away. The problem was that he moved with her. Each step she took back he took forward, until the counter blocked her retreat. "I'm not surprising," she protested grimly. "I'm not intriguing. I'm really boring. I work, I eat, I sleep, I work some more."

"Alone?"

"What?" She was having trouble concentrating when he moved so close their bodies were touching. She flinched away from his plundering hands, but he paid no attention as he slipped the scarf from her hair. Threading his fingers through shoulder-length tresses, he arranged them over her shoulders, every move a subtle caress.

"Do you sleep alone, Jennifer? Or is there someone who tangles his hands in your hair to draw your mouth to his?"

"That's none of your business."

He was closer, his body curving to hers, leaving no doubt that whatever he thought of her now and in the past, his thoughts were fused with desire. "Isn't it a husband's business to wonder about his wife's lovers?"

Jennifer tried to laugh her scorn, but the sound was only a soft gasp. "You're asking questions you gave up the right to ask."

Placing her palms against his shoulders, she shielded her breasts from the crush of his chest. Naked beneath her blouse, she strained even harder to deny herself the very caress her body craved. Her wretched act of denial only succeeded in bringing her into more intimate circumstance.

"Dammit, Mac!" Her cry was complete frustration. With him. With herself. "You have no right!"

"No?" His drawl was a bewildering mix of irony and paradox.

"You gave it up ten years ago."

"Then I was a fool. Being a fool at twenty-four doesn't mean that I must be one at thirty-four, does it?" His fingers tangled in her hair exactly as the phantom lover he'd suggested. He was drawing her closer, his breath a whisper against her lips. "Or that I shouldn't want your kiss as much as you want mine."

Jennifer tore her gaze from his. Her look settled on her hands, pale against the dark indigo of his shirt as they curled over the heavy muscles of his shoulders. She knew the slightest pressure would move him aside. All it would take was one move, yet she didn't make that move. She couldn't. After what seemed an eternity she returned her gaze to his. The lie she wanted to believe caught in her throat. "All I want is for you to leave."

"All, Jennifer? Is that truly all? You really don't want this?" His lips brushed hers, nibbling, caressing. Once, twice, retreating only to return again. His arms were about her. His injured left hand stroked her back, his right hand cradled her head. His eyes were open, watching, engaging, waiting. His tongue touched the sensitive corner of her mouth, and he went utterly motionless at her startled gasp. But only for the space of a drawn breath and skittering heartbeat.

And still those riveting blue eyes beguiled, and his canny mouth seduced.

Jennifer shuddered, the quaking traveling the length of her, and he knew he'd won. Gathering her closer, until their clothing no longer seemed to exist, he murmured, "Admit it, Jennifer, you want me as much as I want you. There are no yesterdays and no tomorrows. We have no history, no future.

"This is another time." He kissed her eyes closed, teasing his own lips with the spiked veil of her lashes. "Another place." His mouth trailed over the soft, smooth curve of her cheek to her mouth. He nibbled at her lips, drawing the full lower lip to the soothing sweep of his tongue, to suckle and stroke. He was a thirsting man, drinking, seeking the quenching that would never come.

After a great length of time he muttered against the soft flesh of her throat, "Another time, Jennifer. Another place, and nothing matters but that you want me."

"This is wrong." She clung to him, his shirt crumpled in her fists. "Too much has happened. Too much has changed."

"It isn't wrong." This time there was no irony, no paradox. "No matter what has happened or what has changed, you're still my wife. I'm still your husband." He lifted her chin, holding her willingly captive. Then softly, so softly she might have imagined it, "And you do want me."

Her lashes dipped to her cheeks, her breath was drawn in short, staccato rhythm, as she released fistfuls of indigo. Her palms slid slowly up his chest, around to his nape, to his hair. Her grasp was hard, demanding. "Damn you, McLachlan," she muttered. "Damn you for coming here. For this."

With a wild, low cry she drew his mouth back to hers. Surrender. To Mac, to desire as passionate as her denial. The floodgates were open. Weeks, months, years of suppressed passion poured out. He held her close, she held him closer. His mouth opened over hers, she met the intimate caress with her own. She was a mindless creature, unthinking, only feeling, basking in emotions she hadn't known for what seemed a lifetime.

She heard a soft, pleading moan and realized too late it was her own. When he laughed, a tender, triumphant laugh, and called her kitten, she felt the flush of countless memories burning in her breast. When he brushed his hands over her hair and kissed her eyelids, she felt the tears for the lost years begin.

When he moved away, leaving a coldness between them, she shivered and opened her eyes. To hide the betraying glitter, she turned her face away.

With her chin between thumb and forefinger he turned her back to him. Catching a tear on his fingertip, he brought it to his lips. "Why the tears, love?"

"I don't know." A quick shake of her head. "I don't know."

"I think you do. You're feeling what I feel, something so beautiful it hurts, so wonderful you hate every minute we've lost. Something that makes you want me as much as I want you."

"I don't!" Her voice broke, reducing her fierce denial to a whisper.

"Ahh, Jennifer, sweet, stubborn Jennifer, after that, can you truly say you don't want me?"

Jennifer dared not avert her gaze. She had to make him believe. "I don't want you." She fought back a shudder as she brazened through the lie. "This was a backlash, an emotional reaction from my day, from the scare in the park. Tonight I felt the shadow of my own mortality. Your kiss denied it."

"Little liar," he said again, the pad of his thumb circling the hint of a cleft in her chin. "If it weren't so early, with another tough day ahead for you, I'd show you exactly how *little* you want me. But I've complicated your life enough for one night." He sighed regretfully and stepped back. "I should go while I still can."

He moved through the room like a jungle cat on the hunt, every sleek muscle in concert with the next. A handsome, dangerous marauder who would have his quarry. At the door, his parka flung over his shoulder, the bandaged hand resting lightly against it, he faced her. "I didn't intend this, but I can't apologize. I'm not sorry it happened."

"Why can't you just go away, Mac? What do you want?"

"I don't know. I don't know why I can't leave, and I don't know what I want. But I will. Before I leave Barclay, I'll know."

"The past is dead. Leave it alone."

"This has nothing to do with the past, Jennifer. It would have happened if we'd just met. The inexplicable, primal attraction of a man for a woman. And deny it as you will, a woman for a man. If we'd been strangers nothing would've been different. The passion would have been there."

"You're wrong, Mac." Jennifer flung her words at him. "It was comfort that I needed. Not passion. Not you."

Mac smiled indulgently. "If this was an example of not wanting me, sweetheart, I hope you never do." With a jaunty salute that flashed the immaculate bandage, he opened the door and stepped through.

"This is absurd! You can't just waltz back into my life as if you'd never been away. As if..." Jennifer bit off her words, for she was talking to a door.

She glared at the spot where he'd been, angry, confused, a little crazy. He'd turned her into a flake, a lunatic, a witless yo-yo.

She didn't understand him. She didn't understand herself.

She wanted him to go. She wanted him to stay.

She was hostile. Guilt transformed it to regret.

She was aloof. He kindled desire.

There were things she must tell him. Her heart couldn't deal with them.

Until he'd come she'd found a restless peace. Now she knew it wasn't peace at all.

"But it would have served, McLachlan," she muttered, turning away from the specter of the man who had been her life and her destruction. "Damn you, it would have served."

Now she knew it never would again.

Five

——

Mac prowled the close quarters of his temporary lodging. The small condo was sufficient for his immediate needs, but he was a man accustomed to open spaces. He'd lived his life in mountains, deserts and jungles, unfettered by more than sky and earth. Walls were temporary containment. Cities, and what were considered their amenities, a passing part of his work.

When circumstances demanded, he'd spent whatever time he had to within the urban atmosphere. For short periods, he learned to enjoy it. But not on nights like this, when his world crowded too closely. When mysteries and problems and unresolved emotions seethed. When he became a caged animal, restive, brooding, ranging his man-made prison with explosive energy.

For years he'd cultivated an ability to adapt, to sleep anywhere, anytime. He was that rare person who could empty his mind of troubles, great or small, merely annoying or life-threatening. Curled on the damp, steaming soil of the jungle floor, or in a windbreak high above the tree line, he could sleep deeply and wake within an hour totally refreshed. A gift, one envied by his colleagues.

On this winter's night his bed waited, cold, lonely. On this night he wouldn't sleep. He knew himself too well to try.

With a derisive grunt he sprawled in a chair. Red-eyed and unshaven, he stared through a dusty window at the paling of a dark sky. If he knew himself so well, why hadn't he found an explanation for why he'd gone where he'd gone, done what he'd done? He raked a hand through his hair, wondering why he'd needed so badly to kiss Jennifer.

The move, repeated a dozen or more times in the last hours, ultimately loosened the bandage on his hand. As it dangled from his wrist, he ripped the last tattered length of it free, flinching at his own rashness as tape removed a band of hair from the back of his hand.

Flexing his fingers, he watched the raw, angry scratches move as skin stretched over tendons. A battle scar, and, oddly, he was proud. Not of himself, but of Jennifer. A woman who walked with courage and confidence where men and women of greater physical size and strength feared to go.

His wounds were symbolic of her courage and vivid testament to her spirit, but he was thinking of her profession, not the park. He hadn't ventured farther into the hospital than the canteen and Jennifer's office, but he had no trouble imagining the strength needed to brave the sad, hopeful faces of children who hurt.

Each day she walked into a lion's den, offering her heart and mind to be savaged. Each day she emerged with her head high, her own hurt hidden.

Hurt never shared. Solace for it never sought, beyond the serenity of the deserted park. His hand closed reflexively, but he ignored the twinges of warning as the taut skin threatened the first quiescent stage of healing. This was the woman he had kissed. This was the woman he wanted.

The dilemma he wrestled with for hours was resolved.

Leaning forward, he took a worn wallet from a small table. In it there was currency in small denominations, the registration for his car, his license, a credit card and a small protective packet of photographs. The latter, worn and tattered at their edges, were the definition of his life. No matter what else he took or left behind, these went where he

went. Other men might play solitaire, using the cards to keep
the loneliness at bay. These were his comfort. In the isola-
tion of his years away from home, he surrounded himself
with those he loved.

This was not South America, and his family was nearby,
but old habits die hard. He took the precious images from
the packet one at a time, laying each carefully on the table
before he took out the next.

First was Dare, nearly eighteen years his senior, as much
father as brother. At twenty he'd given up his education to
take in a trio of strange boys who were his half brothers. For
them he faced down John McLachlan, their drunken father and only common bond. For the family he forged of
them, Dare carved a small empire from a rocky dirt farm.

Mac smiled down at the photograph. Dare hadn't
changed. Through the years he'd been the steadying force
in all their lives. There were strands of silver in the dark hair
now, and the lines around his midnight eyes were deeper, but
Dare was still the strength of the McLachlans. Laying the
picture aside, Mac knew he always would be.

Next was Ross, nine years younger than Dare, with the
same uncanny eyes, the same McLachlan look. If Dare was
the force and strength of the family, Ross was its heart, its
courage. As a skinny, gangly kid without a mother, he'd
coped with life on squalid streets of more cities than he
wanted to remember, and with the vagaries of a drunken
father. In the end, it was he who first shouldered the double responsibility of the newest progeny of John Mc-
Lachlan.

Mac owed his life and his brother's life to Ross. Without
Ross there would be no Mac, no Jamie, perhaps no family.
The story had become legend, of Ross standing in the massive stone barn of the McLachlan farm, scrawny, ragged,
with twin boys tied in the rusty wagon at his heel. Ross who,
with a silent look of pride and courage, challenged Dare not
to see the powerful resemblance, not to want the ragtag band
who were the brothers he never knew he had. Challenging
Dare, at twenty, to be less man than a scrawny eleven-year-
old already was.

Ross, with a man's heart, a man's code, long before his time. A man still.

The last was Jamie, more than a brother, more than his twin, a reflection of his heart and soul. Not identical, but with family traits so compelling few would believe they were not. Jamie was the mischief, the fun, the life. The gifted one. With the body of a woodsman and the hands of an angel, he was steadfast and loyal, as stubborn as Dare, as honorable. His music, moving and haunting, soared straight from his heart.

Jamie, a charismatic mix of masculinity and artistic sensitivity, an eligible but elusive bachelor, a fascinating phenomenon on the concert stage. Yet no matter how distant the paths of their lives, the bond remained. Each was forever a part of the other.

Jamie. Brother, twin, friend.

Next were the McLachlan women, whose strength and honor rivaled that of their men.

Jacinda: First to break the masculine barrier. Who left Atlanta for Madison, turning her own life upside down for Tyler, a child not her own. Who gave to Dare the love he never expected and a second set of McLachlan twins.

Antonia: Beautiful, ambitious. Ross's nemesis, then his savior in a plane crash in an isolated mountain wilderness. An acclaimed actress who ultimately turned her back on fame to be Ross's love and his wife.

Laying aside the photograph, Mac took up another, spending a smiling moment remembering Dare's children. Tyler, an adopted son, loved by Dare as his own, and all the more because he brought Jacinda to Madison. After Tyler, there were the twins. Paul and Amy, carbon copies of their father, with indelible traces of Jacinda's temperament and talents. Three good kids at seventeen and eleven.

With the likenesses of his family spread before him, he sat, a photograph still in his hand. The last, his reason for taking out the treasured packet on this long, sleepless night. Sighing softly, he drew it from the clear square that protected it from the elements and the sweat of his labor. It was older than the rest, the edges more frayed, the image faded, but clear as he laid it on the table.

Jennifer as she'd been. A golden girl, with gold in her flowing hair, her warm brown eyes, tinting the tan of her skin. Golden in the rewards of life and ability. Too young and too sheltered to be the woman he expected and needed. Too naive, for all her worldliness, to understand that love could hurt as nothing else could.

But, God help him, so beautiful, so beguiling.

Always before he'd only to look at her likeness to hear her teasing laughter and remember her maddening touch. Tonight there was no laughter, no haunting memory. At long last they were still, silenced by the woman she had become.

He was free of an obsession. Freed by Jennifer. She was still a mystery to be solved, but not as an old flame, as a stranger. An intriguing and desirable stranger. The slate was clean, old emotions put to rest. What he felt would be honest, fresh.

With a sweep of his hand Mac gathered up the pictures, his game of solitaire done. Perhaps for the last time. His family was only a few hours away. He had seen them recently and would see them again soon. He was home to stay. Neither ambition nor heartbreak would drive him away again.

One by one, he returned the photographs to the pack. Jennifer's was the last, without ceremony, with no lingering regrets. The queen of broken hearts was no more.

Dawn was breaking when he returned the wallet to its place and rose from his chair. There was one more thing he needed to settle in his mind, and one simple telephone call should do it.

Flipping through his address book, he found the name he sought, dialed the corresponding number and waited with little patience. When a grumpy, familiar voice grunted a hello, he began without preamble. "When you recommended me for this project, did you know that Jennifer was here, Rick?"

"Mac?" Rick Casson's usually sharp mind was befuddled by being plucked abruptly from the midst of deep sleep.

"Who else calls you from your bed to ask about Jennifer?"

"Nobody, but . . . my Lord! It's five o'clock in the morning. Nobody in his right mind gets up at five o'clock."

"Maybe I'm not in my right mind." After a beat Mac admitted, "Or maybe I am for the first time in a long time."

"If this call is any indication, I'm not so sure."

"Answer the question, Rick. Did you know Jennifer was here?"

The line was silent for so long that Mac had begun to think Rick had fallen back to sleep. Then he answered, "I knew."

"You knew our history, you knew she was here, so why did you recommend me for this particular job?"

Rick groaned, and Mac knew he was just realizing that if he wanted any more sleep he might as well answer and be done with it. "I only saw her once, years after graduation. Karen and I were astonished at what she'd done with her life after the two of you parted."

"That doesn't tell me why you sent me here."

"Karen and I were still together, but things were beginning to come apart. I remember wishing at the time that I could hear in her voice what I heard in Jennifer's when she asked about you."

"What did you hear?"

"Good Lord! I can't explain that, Mac. It's not something you could put your finger on. A sort of wistfulness, a sadness. Hell, man! I don't . . . know. It was just there, I felt it. And, dammit, it was something I didn't hear from my own wife. But I can tell you this, Mac. It was the same thing I heard in your voice. The same thing I saw in your face the few times our paths crossed on your rare trips home."

"I never asked about Jennifer."

"After a while you didn't. That in itself spoke volumes."

"So, when I came back, looking for work . . ."

"The Barclay project needed you." Rick took up the narration. "You needed it."

"And Jennifer was there."

"Yes," Rick admitted. "Jennifer was there."

"On the strength of one meeting you saw something that led you to throw us into each other's path so you could watch the fireworks?"

"I haven't been watching, but I've been waiting to hear what I hoped would be good news. You two belong together. You just met too soon, before either of you were ready for what came next."

"So you thought if we could meet again . . ."

"And begin again, as if the past never happened."

"It happened."

"No one can deny that. But people change, Mac. They grow. They become other people, and the past can be forgotten."

"What you saw in one meeting made you feel so strongly about this?"

"That, and the firm belief the two of you were destined to be together, except destiny screwed up and you met too soon."

"Destiny? If I didn't know you were clean, that Rick Casson was always clean, I'd ask you what you were smoking."

"If this is hogwash, why did you call?"

Mac made a muffled sound. "I don't know why I called, unless it was to hear exactly what you've said."

"Now you've heard it."

"Yeah."

"So, what're you going to do?"

"Play it as it goes."

"But you do want the new Jennifer."

The line was silent again. Then, "I want her. I don't know why, or for how long, but I want her."

"Then good luck, buddy. Invite me to the wedding."

"We're already married."

"Then invite me to the christening of your first child."

"Jumping the gun a bit, aren't you?"

"Maybe, but we'll see."

"Good night, Rick."

"Good morning, Mac."

The receiver clattered down. His questions had been answered. Rick's view that he and Jennifer were destined to be but the time frame had been wrong was uncanny in how it paralleled his own. But did destiny intend a day, a week, a month? A lifetime?

It was in the hands of fate. Perhaps this time fate would be kinder.

Dawn was more than an allusion now. Clouds that were black, then gray, were etched against the fading sky by deep red that edged into vermilion, then to fiery orange. He could almost hear the throbbing hush of a world waiting for the sun. There was time to catch a few minutes of sleep, but Mac did not seek his bed. Instead, he watched and waited, eager for a new day.

Jennifer was late. Acknowledging greetings with a wave, she hurried to her office. The smile on her face was fixed, a parody of its usual warmth. She hadn't slept well of course, and today she was faced with the task of reprimanding Sally. An unpleasant chore, but one that had to be done. Sally was the soul of discretion in matters dealing with the practice. She would be reminded that the same consideration needed to be given to the little she knew of Jennifer's private life.

Jennifer had been gearing up her resolve all morning. Her speech was imprinted on her mind as she pushed through the double doors that faced Sally's desk. Jennifer stopped abruptly. Sally was always at her desk waiting with a genial greeting and the calendar of her appointments for the morning.

Today Sally's desk was unmanned. The usual sepulchral quiet was broken by the buzz of excited conversation punctuated by spurts of laughter. The location and the source of the disturbance was not difficult to discover. A cluster of student nurses, aids and secretaries was gathered at the window that looked toward the site of the new building.

One hand on her hip, briefcase in the other, Jennifer waited, her foot tapping her impatience, certain someone would sense her presence. Laughter accompanied by intermittent giggles spilled through the room. Jennifer cleared her throat and waited.

When gasps were followed by a spate of applause, her curiosity got the better of her. Setting her case on Sally's desk, she went to the window. As one young woman after another recognized her, they turned and stepped back, parting a path to the window. Only Sally didn't turn, her attention riveted on a giant of a man who hopped and skipped, twirling through a series of intricate and unbelievably fluid moves over steel beams six stories above the ground.

"Good grief!" Jennifer bit back her horror, her fist clasped over a somersaulting heart. "Who is that, and what does he think he's doing?" she demanded when she recovered from the spectacle of a grown man with huge booted feet capering as gracefully as Baryshnikov on beams that, from her vantage point, seemed no wider than cables.

Sally didn't answer or look away from the window until the performance was finished with the flourish of an imaginary plumed hat, a courtly bow and a jaunty wave. The beam was deserted when she faced her employer. "That was Tiny."

"Tiny," Jennifer echoed with a nod. Of course, the odds were in favor of such a goliath being called Tiny. "Is he trying to commit suicide, or is he just plain crazy?"

"He was dancing."

"Dancing!" Jennifer struggled to calm her voice. "Six floors above the ground? Has it occurred to anybody that if he should fall, he would die?"

"Tiny won't fall." There was proprietary pride in Sally's pronouncement. "He might trip over his feet on the ground, but never on the beams."

Jennifer wanted to tell Sally just how ridiculous she found that statement, but a closer look at her secretary stopped her. "What do you mean, he never falls? Has he done this before?"

Sally was smiling. "He does it all the time. He says it's like flying without a plane."

Jennifer wondered what the crash would be like. "You say he does this all the time. Does that mean he's done it here before?"

"Of course. He's been entertaining the children for weeks."

Jennifer felt completely out of touch. "I didn't know."

Sally touched her arm, patting it as one would a child. "You never know what's happening in the hospital, Dr. McLachlan. Unless it concerns your patients."

Jennifer wanted to deny she was that insular and uninvolved, but Sally was right. She was uncomfortable with the truth, but it was the perfect opportunity to address the subject of gossip and discretion. "Sally—"

"Oh my goodness!" Sally clapped her hand to her face, her mouth drawn down. "I forgot! He's waiting in your office."

"He?" Jennifer glanced at her watch. "I don't have an appointment for an hour."

"Not an appointment. Your husband."

"Mac's waiting in my office? What would he want at this hour?" Jennifer turned to stare at the closed door of her office, as if the answer was written on the varnished wood.

"He said you were expecting him—something about dressing a battle wound, and that you owed him." Sally's bright, curious eyes watched her. "Has he been fighting over you?" Then, before Jennifer could dispel the fantasy, Sally declared in an awed voice, "How romantic."

Jennifer resisted the temptation to bristle. She wondered if she shouldn't just go home, go to bed, then get up and start all over again. As it had begun, there was certainly no hope for this day. "Sally," she began, trying to salvage some dignity from this travesty. "Mac hasn't been fighting over me, and if he had been, it wouldn't be romantic." There was definitely no hope for this day. "But I suppose I should see what his problem is."

"His hand was scratched—"

"Sally," Jennifer interrupted her, "you have work to do. So do I. So do we all." The latter was intended for the women who showed no sign of leaving. Because she couldn't bring herself to face their avid stares a moment longer, she gathered up her case and marched into her office.

"Good morning, Doc." Mac's voice floated past her to the waiting room a millisecond before she slammed the door behind her.

Jennifer closed her eyes and leaned against the door. She could hear the excited buzz of voices from the other room.

"Good morning, Doc," he repeated, with a trace of something she couldn't interpret in his tone.

"Is it?" She opened one eye to peer at him. He was standing by the window, dressed in his standard fashion. Today his jeans were new, his shirt the vibrant purple of royalty. He was exceedingly handsome, exceedingly disturbing. This was not the way she wanted to start her day. "Tell me what's good about it."

"Got up on the wrong side of bed, did you?"

"And if I did?" She straightened and crossed the room, careful to keep her desk between them. Taking up the thermos there, she removed the top and poured coffee into the cup beside it. Remembering her rites of propriety, she lifted her cup in a gesture. "Would you like some?"

"Would it be given more kindly than tea and sympathy were last night?"

"I doubt it." She almost smiled. "I have a penchant for offering you something to drink, don't I?"

"This time Sally beat you to it." A tilt of his head drew her notice to a cup resting on the windowsill. "You still haven't told me what's so bad about this day."

"How about a button lost off my favorite blouse, a snag in a new pair of nylons and a madman dancing outside my office window on a sliver of steel. And you." She set the cup down with a bang. "How does that grab you for a good start toward a bad day?"

This time he chuckled. "Maybe the blouse you're wearing isn't your favorite, but it could be mine."

Jennifer felt the touch of his eyes, as real as if his fingers were tracing the lines of her breast beneath the gauzy cloth. "What does that remark mean?"

"That color, I like it. What do you call it?"

"I call it blue, just like everyone else does."

He was undaunted. "It's more than blue."

"All right, then, it's turquoise."

"A pretty color, turquoise."

"Mac, stop!" Exasperation spilled over.

"The snag in your nylons won't show, unless you cross your legs." His blue gaze roamed over her, falling at last at the hem of her skirt. "You have nice legs, by the way. That should make your day better."

"It does," Jennifer drawled. "Heaps."

"And Tiny is the sanest man I know."

"Of course he is." She picked up a pencil, drumming the tip on the blotter covering her desk. "All sane men jump around hundreds of feet in the air like elephants in tutus. My Lord, what would happen if he should fall?"

"He won't."

"That's what Sally said."

"Sally should know."

Jennifer rapped the pencil, watching minute smudges appear on the virgin blotter. "Why should Sally know anything about this Tiny person?"

"You do keep your head in the sand, don't you, Doc?"

"Sally said that, too, or almost."

"I think what she might've been trying to tell you is that she and Tiny are falling in love. Or perhaps it's only lust. Whichever, they have a case."

The pencil was still. "You've got to be kidding."

"Why so surprised? Because she's big? Tiny's bigger. Because she looks and dresses like a Prussian soldier? Tiny doesn't care. He looks into the hearts of people, not their faces. Haven't you seen the look in your own secretary's eyes? I have, and I barely know her. Who do you think this performance was intended for?"

"Sally says he does it to entertain the children."

"On this side of the building where there are only offices?"

"Oh."

"Yeah, Doc, *oh*. Love or lust, on Tiny and Sally it's magnificent."

"He should stop his silly antics."

"He enjoys entertaining Sally and the kids. Your patients have little in their lives to make them laugh. Tiny does, why should he stop?"

"The children might try to emulate him."

"There isn't a child who's seen him who Tiny hasn't told personally that he or she must *never* try what he does, just as they shouldn't fly from a trapeze or be shot from a cannon. Tiny's an expert, and he makes certain they understand that he is." A dark brow lifted over one heavy-lidded eye. "Any more complaints about Tiny?"

Jennifer was defeated. "I suppose not."

The pencil rose. Before it could descend to tap its monotonous rhythm, he was there, finally abandoning his stance at the window, catching her hand in his. "Then the only problem left—" he took the pencil from her and tossed it away "—is a prodigal husband with a wounded hand in need of your attention."

Letting her gaze sweep over their joined hands, Jennifer saw that the scratches were inflamed. "I gave you some ointment and dressing." The instant the words left her lips she recalled that she hadn't. He'd kissed her and she'd forgotten everything. Just as she could forget everything now, as the warmth of his touch seduced her.

Recoiling from her own vulnerability, she drew herself more perfectly erect. The posture, the poised, level gaze, the quiet, calm voice, were part of a cool professional shield. It would be her best defense now. Against herself. "I'm sorry, I guess I forgot. I'll call down and arrange for a nurse to dress your hand."

She was all business, the serious physician to the hilt, but when she would've moved away, Mac kept her, his fingers twining through hers. "Are you sure you want to do that?"

Jennifer flexed her fingers within his grasp. She tried to read his thoughts, but his look was noncommittal. "Is there a reason I shouldn't?"

"Stop and think. The word is out that I'm your husband. These are scratches. Women are more likely to scratch than men." He clucked his tongue, shaking his head in mock regret. "What a field day the rumor mill will have with this little tidbit."

"This sounds like blackmail."

Mac was the epitome of innocence. "Just pointing out the inevitable and the alternative."

Jennifer narrowed her eyes, the lashes nearly obscuring the glint in them. "The alternative being that I should bandage your hand so the entire hospital won't be speculating on who inflicted the wounds and why?"

"Exactly. Except the 'who' is a given." He shook his head again, woefully, fooling no one. "No doubt at all. 'Why' will be the bone of contention."

Drawing her hand from his, she rolled her eyes heavenward, a supplicant in need. "You win. It's no big deal." Moving around her desk, she leaned over the intercom.

"Don't."

Jennifer stopped with her finger hovering over the machine.

"You're going to have Sally call down for gauze and ointment, aren't you."

"I'm a psychologist, Mac. Psychologists don't make a habit of dressing injuries. Because we don't, I haven't stocked such supplies in my office." On the heels of a take-it or leave-it gesture, she said levelly, "You want your hand dressed before work. I have to have Sally order what we need from supply."

"Not this time." From the back side of a chair he produced a paper bag. "I brought some of everything you used last night."

Jennifer sat heavily in her chair, her head in her hand. "You brought your own. Somehow, I should've known you would."

"Just protecting your reputation, darlin'."

"My reputation doesn't need protecting." The calm she'd managed only seconds before eluded her. "Dammit, Mac! If you brought the supplies, why didn't you bandage your hand yourself?"

"Jennifer! Surely you know lefties are notoriously inept." Mac dumped the contents of the bag on the desk and took the seat across from her. His grin was as mischievous as she remembered. "Ready when you are, Doc."

She wasn't ready. Not when a touch could recall his kiss so vividly. "Shouldn't you be on the job, or somewhere?"

"The crew started an hour ago, but just last night an excellent physician strongly suggested I shouldn't work with this unprotected."

Caught in a dilemma of her own making, Jennifer capitulated. "You're right of course." Pushing back from her desk, she shrugged out of her blazer, rolled up her sleeves and gathered up his small infirmary. "Shall we begin?"

Minutes later, Mac's hand had been soaked, medicated and bandaged. Jennifer secured the last strip of tape. "That should do it, so long as you don't sift dirt through your fingers."

Mac stroked the soft gauze of his bandage absently. "I do that occasionally, judging the makeup of the soil."

"I know." Jennifer was too busy putting away what was left of his supplies to catch his surprised glance.

"You do?"

"I saw you do it once, wandering the site alone on a rainy day. I didn't know it was you. The resemblance was there, but it never occurred to me that our paths would cross."

"I'd like for our paths to cross again tonight." At her questioning look, he explained, "To thank you, I'd like to take you to dinner."

"That won't be necessary."

"I know it isn't necessary. I said I'd *like* to take you to dinner. It would be an opportunity to relax together. Something I think we would both enjoy. There's a cozy little place where the crew goes. Tiny and Sally will be there."

It was on the tip of her tongue to say no, but after weeks of avoiding him, suddenly she didn't want to anymore. "I'd like to go to your little place, Mac. I'd like to spend some time with Sally and Tiny, and get to know Tiny better. For that matter, I'd like to know Sally better."

"Then I'll be back for you at, say, six?"

"Make it seven. This promises to be a long day."

When he walked to the door, Jennifer walked with him. He was late for work, yet he was in no hurry to leave. Beneath the banter of the morning, she sensed there was something on his mind. When she let herself question what it was, a trill of fear fluttered in her gut, and she wondered if it was not sheer madness to have dinner with him.

"I've done some soul-searching since last night." He touched her face, tracing the line of her jaw to the cleft of her chin with the pad of his thumb.

As he stroked the curve of her bottom lip, she forgot about madness and fear. "You did?" she whispered, not really sure what she said or why. His touch captivated, but his eyes mesmerized. In the night they always seemed too dark to be blue. Morning light gave lie to the night. McLachlan eyes, he'd told her. Eyes that grew darker with the years. Magnificent eyes.

"What were you thinking, Mac?"

"About us. About now."

"Your conclusions?"

His thumb slid under her chin, lifting her face as he bent to her. He didn't take her in his arms. Only his lips touched hers lightly. Drawing away only inches, he murmured, "I'll tell you tonight."

Jennifer had no breath for words.

"Do me a favor?"

A nod, as she recovered. "If I can."

"Wear your hair free."

"All right."

"And this." With a skill that would astonish her when she was thinking straight, he opened the buttons of her blouse, stopping at the lacy edge of her bra. "Jeans would be better than the skirt, but I don't suppose you have any here at the hospital. No matter." He kissed her again quickly. "You really do have nice legs.

"Seven sharp, sweetheart." With a tug that nearly dislodged the scarf that held back her hair, he was gone.

Jennifer was thankful she was back at her desk before she realized what she'd done. With her knees shaking and her heart tripping over itself, she wondered how she could survive the night.

Six

———

At seven, as promised, Mac rapped on her door.

More pleased than she wanted to admit, Jennifer sighed and, just for a moment, closed her strained eyes. Sally had finished for the day at five, and as she did every weekday, Jennifer spent the next two hours reading charts and reports. With constant glances at the clock, she'd plodded through a ridiculous stack of official forms. A bureaucratic blizzard she refused to allow to encroach on her time with the children.

Feeling rescued from a paper avalanche, Jennifer put away the last form for the day and went to let him in. Turning the key, she stepped back, allowing the door that was always locked when she was alone in the office to swing open. If she was unprepared for the Mac who stood in the waiting room, she was equally unprepared for his reaction to her.

He laughed. After recovering, so did Jennifer. Until he looped an arm around her shoulders and kissed the top of her head.

"You took me at my word." He admired her hair flowing to her shoulders, the blouse not so demurely buttoned and snug jeans just short of ancient. "You look wonderful."

"So do you. I assume the trousers are silk."

"And the jacket. And the shirt." Mac grinned as he plucked at creamy silk visible beneath the lapels of a classic tweed. "I thought you'd be more at ease if I dressed a little less casually."

"I spent my lunch break rushing home for jeans." Tossing her hair from her face, she contemplated their disparate attire. "So, which one of us changes?"

"Neither. We make a handsome couple exactly as we are."

"In that case, I'll get my purse and some papers I need to take home, then I'll be ready."

Mac stood while she slipped into her blazer, collected her purse and a folder from her desk. "Homework?"

"The chart of a new patient. A sixteen-year-old athlete."

He tapped her lips with a forefinger. "No shoptalk. Tonight we're free spirits with no worries."

"I'll buy that," Jennifer agreed. When he swung an arm about her shoulders again, she tucked a thumb in a belt loop at his back. Like old friends they walked together down deserted corridors to the office elevator, to her car and, ultimately, to A Cozy Little Place.

"Yo! Doc, a beer this time?" Tiny raised his voice a decibel above the blare of the jukebox.

"No thanks. I'd better stick to soft drinks. One beer and I'd be out of it, and I have a report to read tonight."

A Sally that Jennifer scarcely recognized scowled across the table at her. "You're going to spend the night studying the Keller boy's report," she accused.

"I have to, Sally. Jason's going to be a tough one." Thoughts of the boy nagged at her. Even as she listened to the raucous banter of the crew and admired the soft prettiness their teasing brought to Sally's usually stern face. Holding the dark, worried thoughts at bay, she could see that Mac was right. The relationship developing between Sally and the giant called Tiny was splendid.

"Sal tells me the way you do it they're *all* tough." Tiny patted her hand with a clumsy paw. "It hurts to wear your heart on your sleeve, but the nicest people do it."

Jennifer smiled at the big ugly man. The subtle tribute meant even more coming from him. In the course of the evening, she'd learned he was an incorrigible and unrepentant busybody, but a kind one. An unvaryingly good-natured man whose tender heart was as big as the rest of him. "Thank you, Tiny, that means a lot."

She was rewarded with a blush and a shy smile. "You just take care of yourself, Doc. For us, as much as the kids." The smile moved to Sally, transforming to unabashed devotion. "Then maybe my Sal won't worry so much."

Jennifer blinked hard. "I'll try, Tiny, I promise."

"Speaking of taking care, that's my cue." Content to listen and observe, Mac spoke for the first time in a while. Jennifer was as relaxed as he'd ever seen her. Natural, without pretense. He was pleased when she was the first to breach the invisible line separating the professionals from the rowdy hard hats. There wasn't a man in the room who wouldn't jump to do her bidding, but he was the man who would take her home.

Skimming his fingers down her arm, he took her hand. A new bandage, expertly done by Mac at the end of his shift, cried fraud to his pose of maladroit lefty. A conspicuous flash of white against his weathered skin, the band of gauze and tape had been explained to the crew with an evasive version of the truth—a scratch, his own stupidity—then ignored.

Mac ignored it now. "Ready?"

"Aw, c'mon, Mac!" A burly fellow rivaling Tiny in size protested. "The evening's young."

Mac laughed. "You're a success, Doc. These guys are so taken by your charm they'd keep you here all night."

Jennifer nearly strangled on the last sip of her drink. With a toss of her tumbled hair and a glance at faded jeans and scruffy sneakers, she sputtered, "This is charm?"

Without blinking an eye, Mac confirmed it. "Yes, charm. Because of it every one of us would like you to stay. But since every one of us also knows you're going to read that

NO RISK, NO OBLIGATION TO BUY...NOW OR EVER!

GUARANTEED

PLAY "ROLL A DOUBLE" AND GET AS MANY AS FIVE FREE GIFTS!

HERE'S HOW TO PLAY:

1. Peel off label from front cover. Place it in space provided at right. With a coin, carefully scratch off the silver dice. This makes you eligible to receive two or more free books, and possibly another gift, depending on what is revealed beneath the scratch-off area.

2. Send back this card and you'll receive brand-new Silhouette Desire® novels. These books have a cover price of $2.99 each, but they are yours to keep absolutely free.

3. There's no catch. You're under no obligation to buy anything. We charge nothing – ZERO – for your first shipment. And you don't have to make any minimum number of purchases – not even one!

4. The fact is thousands of readers enjoy receiving books by mail from the Silhouette Reader Service™ months before they're available in stores. They like the convenience of home delivery and they love our discount prices!

5. We hope that after receiving your free books you'll want to remain a subscriber. But the choice is yours – to continue or cancel, anytime at all! So why not take us up on our invitation, with no risk of any kind. You'll be glad you did!

NOT ACTUAL SIZE

You'll look like a million dollars when you wear this lovely necklace! Its cobra-link chain is a generous 18" long, and the multi-faceted Austrian crystal sparkles like a diamond!

report tonight come hell or high water, I'd better get you home.''

A chorus of groans rose from the table by the booth they shared with Sally and Tiny. "Sorry, guys." Jennifer grinned at the rough, hard men who treated her as if she were precious and fragile. "Duty calls."

"You'll be back, won't you, Doc?" The voice called from a crush of more hard, fit bodies she'd than ever seen assembled in one room.

"Count on it," she said to the group as a whole. With a final wave she followed Mac from the booth and slipped into the coat he held.

When she moved to pull her hair free, he was a step ahead, letting her hair drift like falling light to the shoulders of her navy blazer before taking her arm. "Ready?"

With invitations to come again ringing in her ears, Jennifer left the club, realizing she couldn't remember when she'd enjoyed an evening more.

"I thought when you called the restaurant a cozy little place, you were describing it, not naming it." Jennifer walked the path that meandered through her back lawn. Jason Keller's reports waited on her desk. But her hand was tucked in the curve of Mac's arm, and after weeks of cold weather, the night was balmy and too beautiful to miss.

"Its name describes it."

"Some of the hospital staff were there, but your friends have made it their home away from home."

Mac made a distracted sound and drew her to a stop. "I'm glad you liked the crew and they liked you. But you don't really want to waste the rest of this lovely night replaying the happenings at A Cozy Little Place, do you?"

"You're right, I don't."

"Can you spare a few minutes away from Jason Keller?"

"A few, but only that." Jennifer wished she never had to face the report that lay waiting. Never had to face the frightened adolescent.

Mac drew her into his arms and was content to hold her. Throughout the evening she'd bewitched him. With perceptions honed to an exquisite intensity, he'd been aware of everything about her. The tiny quirk of her lips before she smiled. The way she touched the tip of her tongue to her full lower lip when she concentrated. Her breasts veiled in turquoise, rising in hearty laughter. The masculine leather belt that accentuated a hand-span waist. The curve of slender hips, the length of shapely legs gliding in faded denim.

He saw everything, absorbed everything. Every nuance burned into his mind an indelible reminder that she was a desirable woman. Small things, unremarkable. Unforgettable. Her hair a sparkling mantle on her shoulders. Her fragility. Her strength. The unconscious sensuality that radiated from her, drawing the roughest, most cynical hard hat like a magnet. The kindness, the perfect innocence in her response to their flirting.

Tonight the moon glided through a cloudless sky, its light painting her skin with a spellbinding translucence. She was so still in his arms, so still in the moonlight, he dreaded the fatigue that hovered over like a shadow. Tilting her face to his, he searched for the telltale signs and saw only solemn, biding curiosity.

She was solemn and quiet but tonight she had laughed, truly laughed. And she had gone with him in that mood, willingly and comfortably. Now she waited, keeping her own counsel, letting him take the last of the evening where he would.

Mac wondered if she had any concept of where he would like it to end. That he wanted with all that was in him to draw her to him and, lifting her in his arms, take her to bed.

It would be a mistake. This was a new beginning, and there was much he must know about this woman and she about him before they made love. Her level gaze was reserved, unreadable. He had no idea what she was thinking. Quietly he asked, "Are you afraid, Jennifer?"

A nod, almost indiscernible in the moonlight. "A little."

"Why are you afraid?"

A lie tangled with the truth. "I don't know."

In a move that had become habit, he stroked the curve from her chin to the line of her lips. "Do you trust me?"

"I think so." Then a frown and another nod, this one more positive. "I do. I do trust you. I've always trusted you."

Something stirred in Mac, a weight lifted. A question, uncertain at best, resolved. His fingers threaded through her hair. Loose and free, it shone in the night, and what was heavy gold in the sunlight was misty silver beneath the moon.

She was beauty in the eyes of the beholder, for with trust on her lips she was lovelier to Mac than she'd ever been. He moved a step closer, letting his fingers slip through her hair and away. He did not touch her again as he towered over her. "Would you do something for me? Something simple, even foolish, that I can't explain?"

Her look grew puzzled. "If I can. Just tell me where and when."

"Here. Now."

Jennifer was truly startled then. But with the easy comfort of their evening spent together to soothe her and the warmth of his touch still lingering at her lips, she couldn't deny him. "All right, here and now."

"I'm only going to kiss you, Jennifer." He expected she would refuse him, after all. Instead, she waited, if not calmly, then with a surface poise. "I won't touch you in any other way. You can do anything you wish, except open your eyes."

"Only that?" Jennifer hadn't known what to expect, but it wasn't this. Mac made it impossible to keep up her guard when every move was a surprise.

"Only that. I promise."

"I don't need your promise, Mac. Your word is enough."

He almost broke his word then. Only the honor of a lifetime kept him from taking her back in his arms. Only the knowledge that if he did he wouldn't stop with a kiss sustained that honor. Instead, he began what might be a futile quest.

"First this." With his lips he closed her eyes. One, then the other, his mouth teasing the delicate membrane, brushing over the curtain of her lashes. The silence was so profound he could almost believe he heard the beat of her heart in cadence with the throb of a vein at her throat. Her up-turned face was sculpted in shadow and light. In the disorienting darkness behind her eyelids, there was no equilibrium and her body swayed. A slight, little move, but not even her hand thrown out to grasp his shoulder kept her full woman's body from brushing his.

His jacket was heavy silk, hers supple crepe, but neither disguised the solidity of his chest nor the yielding softness of her breasts. A long moment passed. Jennifer did not step back, did not take her hand from his shoulder. Lashes lay like a fringe of gold against her cheek and her eyes did not open.

Mac stared down at her, his own heart throbbing, measured, hard, leaving a hollow, yearning vacuum between each beat. Slowly, as surely as the drumming of life, he was drawn at last to her lips.

His touch was tender, teasing at her mouth, offering pleasure for the taking. He kissed her. Soft, chaste, teasing. Again and again, in gliding whisper touches, gentle as morning mist upon her skin. A summer wine, warm from the sun, dazzling in its promise, sensual in its innocence.

Jennifer uttered a wordless sound against his lips, both hands clutched at his shoulders. A longing that seethed quietly burst into the pain and pleasure of bittersweet need. Pagan and primitive, it drew her to him. She wanted to be closer. Her hands were at his nape, holding him. Her mouth opened to his, to sip the summer wine of his kiss.

She didn't think of fear, or trust, or of secrets that must be told. She simply lost herself in him. He touched her soul with his kiss, and her body coveted the touch of his hands.

She hurt, she wanted, she needed. Her mouth was wild against his, and her body trembled. She murmured the soft whimpering sounds of a woman's need for a man. "Hold me, Mac. Touch me."

"Jennifer." Only her name, breathed against her skin.

Jennifer shivered, her fingers threaded through his hair. Madness! This was madness. She was lost in a dark world, where every sensation was more shattering than the last. Nocturnal sounds, quiet, secret, blended with human cries. The whisper of a lazy wind high among the treetops. The fall of a pinecone muffled by the carpet of needles from the mother tree. The slide of silk against flesh as Mac moved. The sigh of his breath. These were the thunderous symphony of her night.

Scents, piquant, subtle, drifted in the crisp, clean air. A perfume of trodden grass and fallen leaves. Of a Southern winter. Of evergreen and Mac.

Taste was Mac's kiss on her lips. Touch, the brush of his body as she moved against him. He was everything in her sightless, isolated world.

Everything. And in the darkness he'd invoked, she wanted more. "You made a promise I didn't accept. A promise not taken can't be broken." Her short nails threatened to pierce his scalp. "Touch me, hold me, as if you never had before. We have no history," she murmured, giving back his own words. "There are no yesterdays and no tomorrows. Only now."

Then, mute and beautiful, she waited before him. He wanted to touch her. Dear God! He wanted to hold her.

He was stunned by her reaction and by the desire blazing through him. His thoughts were muddled, his reactions slow and ponderous. When he wanted to sweep her into his arms, dragging her body hard against his own, his would not obey. His arms lifted, numb and weighted. His hand hovered at her shoulder, but would never descend.

In the hush, Jennifer drew a long, gasping breath. He saw the slow wondering shake of her head. Dismay at what she'd done, what she wanted, was written on her face. A low moan racked her. Sliding her hands over his shoulders to his chest, she crumpled the lapels of his jacket in her fists, as if in frustration she would shake him from his strange inertia.

Shock and confusion warred with resignation and, he hoped, regret, as she sighed softly and, with her arms falling to her side, moved away.

She was pale, as pale as marble in the silvery light. A carved, sightless image with only the ragged rise of her breasts to break her stillness. She had released him from his promise, but kept her own.

"Jennifer—"

"I'm sorry," she interrupted him, with a tense, humorless laugh. "I don't know what I was thinking. You must think I'm mad."

Her words were a kick in the gut. He couldn't stand it an instant longer. "Open your eyes, Jennifer." For a long while he thought she wouldn't. And with a sickening dread he wondered if she couldn't bear the sight of him. "Please," he whispered. "Look at me."

A shadow crossed her face. A cloud that hadn't existed only moments ago ghosted over the moon. Time stopped for Mac. Then, as a veil lifting, her lashes swept from her cheeks. Her somber eyes, deep pools of amber revealing nothing, found his.

What was she thinking? What lay behind that fathomless stare? Did she wonder what he'd hoped to accomplish with this bizarre venture? Did he know himself?

He had no idea what to say. Raking his fingers through his hair, he shook his head. "I don't know what I thought I'd prove with this. I don't know why I did any of it." A half-truth. Mac was too honest for half measures, and Jennifer deserved better. His hand made a path through his hair again before falling away.

He grimaced in disgust at his own deceit. "That isn't true." His voice was strained. "I wanted your complete concentration. As sophomoric as it sounds, I wanted to be the focus of your world. The man I am, not a memory."

"A new beginning?"

"If we can."

"To what end, Mac?"

"I can't answer that." His gaze swept over her, lingering at the thrust of her breasts beneath her jacket. "I want you as a man wants a very desirable woman. Beyond that I can't say."

"Strangers. No past, no guarantees, no future."

"No old flames. No wounded hearts worn on sleeves," he added. "No grieving for what we've lost."

No grieving for what we've lost. An innocent phrase that brought down an avalanche of guilt and grief.

Jennifer shivered, her body clenched in a vice of pain. She was a fool, living a fool's dream. Mac's layman's venture into sensory deprivation had succeeded only too well. His touch, his kiss, had become the center of her world. Making her feel the things she never thought she could feel again. Stirring passions long buried.

For a while she'd forgotten, letting herself believe a new beginning could be. A fool's dream. An impossible dream.

She was visibly distraught. The sudden turnabout had him reaching out to steady her.

Lurching away, she drew back from what she'd craved. "Don't touch me. Not now."

Mac recoiled as if she'd clawed his flesh once more. "Good Lord, Jennifer, what's wrong."

"Wrong?" She shuddered, appalled that she could forget. Appalled at the vulnerability that was betrayal. "Everything's wrong. We've made one mistake, I don't want to make another. I *can't* make another. We should forget tonight."

"Forget?" His tone was brittle. The change in Jennifer was unbelievable, but unmistakable. Confusion and tension gave rise to cold fury. "Perhaps you'll tell me how to do that. Turn it off like a tap? Cold one minute, hot the next, then nonexistent?" The sarcasm was a slow, lazy drawl, but the lips that uttered it were taut. "What do I do, Jennifer? How do I forget you as you've been tonight? Warm, friendly, charming my friends out of their boots. How the hell do I forget that you wanted me as badly as I still want you?"

Jennifer had half turned. She whirled now to face him. There was anger in her. She welcomed it. Full-blown anger, blessed anger that appeased the guilt of forgetting and, for a little while, eased a secret anguish.

"Want?" Her voice was low, derisive, as wintry as her expression. "What does it matter that I want you or that you want me? What does it mean? That we should tumble into bed, forgetting everything?

"Strangers!" She spat the word at him, stepping beyond the bounds of rationality. "Perhaps we were always that, perhaps it's for the best that we always will be. If it's any consolation, your little exercise was successful. I didn't think of the past. I didn't think at all. The man I wanted was the man who held me.

"But no matter how much I want you, no matter how we may have become different people, the past can't be changed or forgotten." There were tears in her eyes, tears he mustn't see. Turning away again, she murmured brokenly, "Some things can't be forgotten. They must not be."

Mac was pale. His voice was deadly quiet. "Why do you still bear my name? Why are you still my wife? And what the hell was tonight all about if you hate me so much?"

"I don't hate you, Mac." When she looked at him the tears she'd meant to hide stained her face. Silver tears, like the cold light of the moon. "I never hated you."

"You'd have a hard time convincing me of that at the moment." Even as he uttered the bitter, sardonic words, he wanted to kiss away her tears. He wanted to protect her and wondered from what. What demons lurked in her soul?

"I won't try." She made no move to brush away the fresh tears that glittered on her lashes.

"I know." Mac slid his hands into his pockets. She didn't want his comfort or his protection. Jennifer wanted nothing from him. "I didn't think you would."

"Good. Then you'll understand if I ask you to leave and not come again." Her eyes flickered to his left hand and away. "You've done an excellent job dressing your hand, but if you should need help, ask Sally to call a nurse. If it weren't for your work, you wouldn't need a bandage at all. And not even then in a day or two.

"There's no reason our paths must cross again, Mac. It's better that way." Her normally direct and level gaze avoided his.

"Better, Jennifer? For whom?"

"For both of us."

"You didn't think so a few minutes ago. Evading me was the last thing you were thinking of."

"A few minutes ago I wasn't thinking at all." Then with a hollow sadness, she murmured, "The evening was a mistake."

"What happened, Jennifer?"

"I just said it," she answered grimly, wearily. "If you insist, I'll say it again. I made a mistake."

"What mistake, Jennifer? And when?"

"Don't be ridiculous," she snapped. "You know that as well as I."

"Do I?" With narrowed eyes he searched her face. The melancholy he'd heard in her laugh weeks ago was mirrored in her eyes. A haunted anguish lay in their depths. "I don't think so." His anger was gone. There was tenderness in his voice. "The mistake was made years ago. And it was mine as much as yours."

"It isn't important what you think." Jennifer was frantic for him to leave. She didn't like the gentle turn his thoughts were taking. She wanted his anger. She could cope with anger. With an indifference intended to drive him away, she said coldly, "Our mistakes are of little consequence now. What happened, or when, doesn't matter anymore. What matters is that it's late, and Jason Keller's report is waiting. What matters is that tomorrow I have to help a young boy, with most of his life ahead of him, face his shattered dreams."

Mac nodded. He didn't believe her, but he wouldn't argue. She was too weary for that. "I'll walk you to your door."

This, another sudden change, took Jennifer by surprise. Mac seemed ever able to keep her off-balance. She drew a long, deep breath, breathing in the soothing, cleansing scents of the night. "That won't be necessary."

"I'll walk you to your door." Nothing would persuade him to leave before he saw that she was safely in her house, the doors locked behind her.

"All right." She would have agreed to almost anything as long as he left. "We'll do it your way."

With her back straight, her step firm on the winter grass, she marched over the lawn, up the stairs to the terrace and to the house. At the door she turned, chin tilted, offering her hand, her arm extended stiffly. "I'll say goodbye now."

"Not goodbye." Mac brushed aside her hand. Clasping her haughty little chin in his palm, he bent to her. This time she did not come alive under his kiss. Her lips were wooden beneath his, enduring what she couldn't avoid. Undaunted, he lifted his mouth only inches. His gaze held hers. "I'll be back. Count on it."

Reaching past her, he opened the door. "Good night."

"Goodbye, Mac," she said firmly.

"Not this time, Jennifer."

She didn't argue. It didn't seem worth the effort. Mac would do what he chose for as long as he was in Barclay. Until his part of the project ended, she would have to cope.

Without another word to him, she stepped through the door and closed it securely behind her. With her back against the door, she listened as his footsteps sounded over the brick terrace and down the walk.

He would be back.

The next morning when she pushed open the double doors leading to the suite that housed her office, Jennifer half expected Sally to greet her from the reception desk with a warning that Mac was waiting in her office.

Instead, Sally's desk was deserted. And the man who waited, folded like an accordion in a chair by her office door, was definitely not Mac.

"Dr. McLachlan?" He sprang from his seat. Rather, he unfolded. Jennifer wondered idly if he was seven feet tall, or only looked it because of his lanky slenderness.

"I'm Dr. McLachlan." Shifting her briefcase, she offered her hand. "What can I do for you?"

"I'm Lincoln Avery." His grasp was firm, his gaze direct. He seemed to assume his name meant something to her.

"I'm sorry, I'm afraid I don't..." At a loss, she let the sentence dwindle away. Where was Sally? Off in another part of the hospital watching Tiny play Baryshnikov on steel? She made a mute and, for Jennifer, ineffectual gesture. "My secretary must be out on an errand."

"I know. I met her earlier. She said something about something little and rushed out. Before she left, she suggested I make myself comfortable. I did." Pausing to catch his breath, he shook his head ever so slightly. "You've forgotten."

He was smiling, perfectly at ease. Not the least insulted that she didn't remember something she obviously should. His eyes were blue, but not so startling as Mac's.

Shrugging aside the damnable comparison, Jennifer searched her mind for reasons she should recognize, if not this poised young man, at least his name. When the memory came, it came like a dash of cold water. "You're Lincoln Avery, the new psychologist!"

"Yes, ma'am."

"You don't look old enough to be Lincoln Avery." Actually, Lincoln Avery was thirty-four. Mac's age and four years her senior. But when one read his résumé, tallying all he'd done, his achievements and accomplishments, one forgot his youth.

"Sorry." Lincoln shrugged and released her hand. "The cherubic mug never seems to bother the kids."

Jennifer realized she was gaping. "It wouldn't of course. Look, why don't we go into my office?"

"If you don't mind, Dr. McLachlan, I'd like to see *my* office and maybe spend a minute getting oriented." He indicated a worn black bag sitting beside his chair, an array of office supplies spilling from it. "Then I'd like to get started."

"You intend to start seeing patients today?"

"Sure. From what your gal Friday tells me, you need help, yesterday." Lincoln folded again, lifting the stuffed bag.

"Actually, yesterday is right, at least figuratively." With a wave, Jennifer communicated that he should follow her. Speaking over her shoulder as she went, she led him past her own office to a second door. Throwing it open, she stepped back and, with another gesture, waved him in. "Your office, Dr. Avery."

He grinned, and she was struck again by his youthfulness. Lincoln settled in the chair behind his desk, spinning it like a top. After a minute he stopped. He was unperturbed that she witnessed this moment of childish delight. Jennifer knew then that the hospital was fortunate that this very gifted Californian wanted a change of location, as well as a change of pace from his private practice. Most fortunate of all would be the children.

"The facilities here are excellent," Jennifer informed him. "But they'll be even better when the new addition is completed."

"I'm sure they will." Lincoln smoothly returned the conversation to a more current concern. "Define 'figuratively.'"

Jennifer's gaze had wandered with her mind to the window and beyond, to the skeletal steel climbing to the sky. And to the man who had walked there in the rain. "I beg your pardon?"

"Figuratively," Lincoln prodded her.

Jennifer turned her back to the window. He watched her expectantly. A brow only a little darker than his sun-streaked hair lifted in a broad parody of curiosity. Mac's darker hair was streaked in much the same way. Bleached by years under the sun.

Realizing that Lincoln was waiting, his curiosity no longer a parody, she put the haunting image from her mind, addressing his question. "By a figurative yesterday, I meant we've been busier than we are at the moment. The hospital census is cyclical. Low before Christmas, a full house after the new year. Then beginning to thin again with the approach of spring. We try to get the children home for the holidays. And spring quite simply seems to be a good time. At least for some. In the autumn it climbs again."

"The census is low now?"

"Dropping."

"Friday says you work hard no matter."

It took a second to assimilate and assign the name while deciphering his verbal shorthand. Lincoln Avery was as direct as his gaze and not a man to waste words. Nor, it seemed, one to take himself too seriously. "Since we'll be sharing her services, you'll find that Sally's a crackerjack secretary. But she does talk too much and she worries too much."

"Maybe the first, Doctor." Keen blue eyes swept over her, not missing the telltale traces of a sleepless night. "I don't think so on the last." Then he grinned, that confident, boyish grin of a mischievous kid who is good at what he does, and loves it. "But I'm here now."

"So you are." Jennifer laughed.

"I'll have to learn the routine, but I'm a fast learner."

Jennifer laughed again and offered her hand. "Welcome aboard, Lincoln. You're just what these children need."

When she returned to the reception area surprisingly cheered and ready to begin her day, Sally was at her desk. The large woman observed her over a pair of half glasses perched precariously on her nose. "Dr. McLachlan, I see you've met the new kid on the block."

"I was thinking more in terms of the marine has landed."

"He has, indeed," Sally drawled, "and made himself perfectly at home."

"He does have a way of doing that. I like him, Sally. He's going to be terrific with the children."

Probing beyond the skillful application of her makeup to the ravages of the night as Lincoln had done, Sally muttered, "A jolly marine, and not a minute too soon."

"I don't want to know what you mean by that sage observation, Sally." Jennifer had decided not to reprimand the woman for her gossip. She knew now that Tiny was Mac's source, not Sally. "Do you have my appointments for the day?"

Sally handed her a list. "Jason Keller's first. He'll be a tough one. But I have some good news."

Jennifer waited. Good news was rare.

"Chrissie Hanyon's in remission."

"Thank God!" This meant the little girl with hauntingly familiar blond hair and deep blue eyes would have a few months of renewed health. "Maybe this is a landmark day. A new associate of Dr. Avery's caliber and news like this about Chrissie. Can you think of anything better?"

"Only that you get a little more rest than it looks like you had last night."

"I don't need much sleep, Sally. By the way—" with a studied casualness she gathered up her briefcase "—has Mac called?"

"Sorry, no."

"It's not important. I wasn't expecting his call." She smiled again at Sally. This time some of the delight was missing.

Alone, behind the closed doors of her office, she struggled to concentrate on Lincoln Avery, and found herself comparing him to Mac.

Seven

Jennifer sat in broken light. Bars of shadow and sun spilled over her chair and the floor, stopping short of the unrelieved white of the narrow hospital bed. Jason Keller lay prone, listlessly watching the creeping light. Jennifer watched Jason, waiting for him to speak.

He was a striking child, taller than most his age, and heavier. The weight in bone and muscle and not an ounce of fat. His body was so mature and developed, it sometimes required conscious effort to remember that he was a child. At the moment, with a bitter scowl drawing his features into an ugly mask, it was as easy to forget he was attractive.

At sixteen, Jason had everything. An exceptional mind, astounding coordination. He was president of his class, captain of the football team. Colleges all over the country were coming to games to see him play. With his mind and talent, and a face perfect for the camera, he was likely a budding millionaire.

There was one problem, and because of it Jennifer could forgive his sullenness, his caustic bitterness, the silence that stretched into precious days.

Jason Keller had cancer.

Jennifer had battered against the stone wall of his silence for days. Until she felt that badgering him only made the situation worse. For two more days she'd simply sat by his bed in silence, hoping he would speak.

Shadows crept over the foot of the bed. She gauged by them that it was time to go. Pursing her lips, she tried to keep the disappointment from her face. Time was running out. If Jason didn't respond, she had no idea what his parents and his surgeons would decide. No one wanted to send a despondent child into the operating room. But was there a choice?

Amputation.

An ugly word. A scary word. A necessary word. A word that shattered the dreams of a gifted young athlete. With it he would never be a college or professional quarterback.

Without it he would not live.

"Jason." Jennifer stood, sliding her pen into the pocket of her lab coat and tucking a report under her arm. "I'm sorry you didn't feel like speaking to me today. Maybe tomorrow?"

"Not tomorrow. Not ever."

She was startled by his words, the first he'd uttered in her presence. Before she recovered enough to respond, bitterness spilled out of the petulant mouth.

"Don't come back, ever. I won't talk to you. You can't help me. Nobody can, but especially not you." Blazing dark eyes turned on her, scorching her with their hate. "What do you know about anything? Did you ever play ball? Did your future depend on playing ball? Was it your life, all you wanted to do?"

Jennifer swallowed, shocked by the hatred she faced. "No, Jason," she answered honestly.

"Have you ever lost anything that meant everything to you?"

Jennifer flinched beneath the lash of his words. Pain, dark and unrelenting, welled inside her. Each breath she drew was like a knife. And even in her pain, she damned herself for being vulnerable to his puerile contempt. She wanted to blame her reaction on frustration, but knew it was more than that. It was the season that was near. The season of her grief.

He was waiting for an answer. "We've all lost something, Jason. We've all hurt. We grieve, then make the best we can of the rest of our lives."

"Sure, lady, sure" the boy sneered. "What did you lose? Your stethoscope? A scarf for your pretty hair?" His hostile eyes swept downward. "I see you never lost a leg." His fists were clenching the edge of the sheet. "What the hell do you know about anything?"

"More than you think."

"Sure you do." His fury turned glacial. "Get out and don't come back. I don't want any prissy doctor who doesn't know a football from a watermelon near me. Nobody can help me, especially not you."

Jennifer lifted an entreating hand, but the boy turned his back on her. The twisted sheet was pulled about his eyes and ears, shutting him away. There was nothing more she could say or do. She'd stood unresponsive when she should have spoken. In her silence she failed Jason Keller.

Forcing herself to walk when she wanted to run, she left the room. In the corridor, she leaned against the wall to steady herself. She hadn't been ready for his questions, nor to answer them honestly. She hadn't faced her own loss, her own grief. How could she help this man-child face his?

"Jennifer?" A consoling hand closed over her shoulder. "That was rough. Are you all right?"

Jennifer looked up, and up a little farther. "Lincoln. You heard?"

Lincoln took his hand away. After a second he shrugged and shoved both hands into his pockets. "The whole floor heard."

"I can't reach him. He won't agree to surgery, and he won't listen. And every day counts."

"He's underage. His parents can take the responsibility."

"Nobody wants to take him to surgery until he comes to terms with it." Jennifer slid her hands beneath her bound hair to tense, knotted muscles. "Who knows how he would react?"

Lincoln knew too well what Jennifer left unsaid. The boy could be suicidal if not handled with kid gloves. "A shame. The hospital scuttlebutt says the kid had a real future."

"He still does," she snapped more harshly than she intended. "There's more for him in this world than playing ball."

With his usual good humor, Lincoln ignored her outburst. "Won't argue that. The kid about to lose a leg might, though."

"Lincoln!" Jennifer caught at his sleeve. "Were you an athlete? Did you play ball?"

A peculiar look crossed the tall man's face. A twinkle glinted in his eyes. "A little." The words were long, drawn out. "Some round ball."

"Round ball?" Her frown cleared almost instantly. "Oh, you mean basketball, as opposed to football."

"Right."

"Then maybe Jason would listen to you!"

"Maybe." He rocked back on his heels, hands still in his pockets, his expression still one she couldn't interpret. "Be worth a try."

"I could take some of your patient load," she bargained. Lincoln had only been in the hospital a week, and already his presence was felt, and his stamina was legend. But fair was fair.

"Won't be necessary. Just one thing."

"Anything."

"I'd like to discuss his case over dinner tonight."

"I'm sorry, Lincoln. I don't think I can."

"I'll see your patient, anyway, Jennifer. But you did promise me anything." He grinned wickedly. "Considering the scope of the promise, you should be delighted it's only dinner I want."

Jennifer laughed. She knew when she'd been bested.

"Expecting someone?"

Jennifer laid down her fork and folded her hands in her lap. "Of course not, Lincoln. Why do you ask?"

"Well, judging by the number of people who've stopped to say hello, I'd say everyone in the world is here. Yet you seem to be watching for someone who isn't."

"I don't know what you mean."

"You've been watching the door all evening, Jennifer."

She was embarrassed she'd been so transparent. When Lincoln maneuvered this dinner date, she hadn't anticipated he would take her to A Cozy Little Place. "I didn't mean to be rude."

"No problem. We've accomplished what we intended. Jason is a torn, bitter kid. He said some vicious things to you, but he was only lashing out in fear. There's a gentleman under all that anger. In normal circumstances he wouldn't hurt you or anyone else. I'm not sure I can reach him, but I'll try. I'll begin tomorrow."

"Are you always like this?" She kept her gaze on him. He wouldn't catch her stealing glances at the door again.

"Like what?"

"So easygoing and practical. I've never seen you take offense."

"I have my days." He brushed aside her compliment. "It's not much fun to be mad or to worry over slights most people didn't intend." He leaned his elbow on the table, resting his chin on his palm. "As luck would have it, while you've made such a determined effort not to be rude by watching the door, I think the fella you've been looking for has arrived."

Her gaze flew to the door. No one was there. "Where?"

Lincoln was as droll and calm as ever. "Don't look, just sit as you are. He's in the corner by the jukebox. Not a tall guy, but then, he's not short, either. His hair is dark, and he looks strong enough to pick up the jukebox and throw it at me. From the way he's glaring at me, he's considering it.

"So—" Lincoln straightened and, reaching across the table, took Jennifer's hand in his "—let's give him something to glare about."

"Lincoln! Are you crazy?" She tried to draw her hand away, but he linked his fingers through hers and drew them to his lips. "You are crazy! You have no idea who I was looking for or if he's glaring at us."

"Oh, he's glaring at us all right. And I'd place bets that he's the one you've had on your mind. You're certainly on his." Lincoln kept hold of her hand. "He's about to pay us a visit."

Panic skittered down her spine on little clawed feet. Only the fervent hope that among Lincoln's many character quirks lay a vivid imagination kept her from lurching from her seat, committing an unpardonable act of cowardice by running for her life. With a sinking feeling, as she watched Lincoln's amused expression, she decided prudence was a better choice of word than cowardice.

Then there was no more time for thinking. *He* was there, by their table, a presence sensed more than seen. Her heart did one of those little somersaults that left an aching void in its wake. Only profound restraint kept her from shivering. Her hand convulsed in Lincoln's, her cold fingers clinging to his like a lifeline. When she gathered the courage to look, a blazing midnight gaze was waiting.

"Jennifer." He inclined his head in greeting. His eyes roamed over her, leaving no part untouched. She might've been a mare on the auction block, her Irish sweater and snug woolen trousers a horse blanket. His hard face softened only when his attention returned to the scarf tied securely at her nape. It seemed to please him that her hair was not loose.

Restive under the blatant inspection, she spoke the first thought that came to mind. "It's been a while, Mac."

His gaze didn't waver. "Eight days."

"Ah, you've counted."

"You haven't?"

She tried to keep her gaze as steady as his and could not. Each time she saw him was a revelation. She always seemed to forget how lean and hard he was. How powerfully built. Flustered, she looked away, damning him for what he could do to her with a look or a word. Reacting in anger, she answered tersely, "I really haven't had time to think about it."

He laughed. The indulgent, intimate laugh one reserved for a much loved but willful child. "Little liar."

Lincoln, who'd been content to watch and wait, sighed heavily. "Look, fella, do you really think you have any right to speak to the lady like that?"

"Lincoln, no—"

"And who might you be?" Mac interrupted Jennifer, turning his piercing stare on her companion.

The taller, more slender man was unperturbed by the menace in Mac's question. As affably as if he was discussing the weather over afternoon tea, Lincoln leaned back in his chair, looking into eyes like a winter night. "There's no 'might be' to it. But since you asked, I'm Lincoln Avery, Barclay's newest staff member, Jennifer's associate. And for tonight, her date."

"Lincoln," Jennifer began, and got no further before Mac interrupted again.

His icy regard swept over their entwined hands and back again to Lincoln's face. "Being her date gives you the right to decide what I should and shouldn't say to her?"

"Damn straight." Lincoln was as loose as ever. There was no threat in his words or his body language. A condition that could change in the flicker of an eye or with an ill-advised word. The challenge was there, an undercurrent. "If she was your date, would it be any different?"

Mac eyes narrowed. Hooking his thumbs in the belt loops of his jeans, he tapped a booted toe. A slow, measured, ominous tap. After a long, considering moment, his head jerked in a single nod. "It would be different."

"You'd knock my block off."

"Damn straight."

"What gives you the right to such drastic measures?"

Mac leaned on the table, palms flat on the gaudy floral cloth, gaze level with Lincoln's. "Not that it's any of your business, Dr. Avery, but for the record, I'm Jennifer's husband."

Lincoln didn't react. His expression barely changed. Something suspiciously like a grin crossed his face, then disappeared. "The long, lost Mac McLachlan. Why doesn't that surprise me?"

"Not lost anymore, Avery."

Jennifer had watched, speechless. Now she found her tongue and her temper. Jerking her hand from Lincoln's, she shoved back from the table. "Who the hell are either of you that you can stand here discussing me as if I were—"

"A beautiful woman we both want," Lincoln supplied helpfully, and succeeded in turning her anger to skyrocketing rage.

"*You* want!" She turned on Mac, then Lincoln, her anger more apparent in the obdurate control in her muttered words. "Have you stopped to consider what *I* want?"

Mac straightened from the table, reaching for her, but she dodged away. With his hand still hovering in the air where she had been, he asked gently, "What *do* you want, Jennifer?"

"I want what I'd finally found before you came back into my life. I want peace and quiet again. With no one making a scene or stirring up memories and grief." Taking her purse from her chair, she regarded both men levelly. "Now, with or without your consent, I'm going home." Her glacial look could have frozen the most foolhardy in his tracks. "And I'm going alone."

"Ouch," Lincoln said a minute after she stalked through the crowd and out the door. Turning to Mac, who was standing as she'd left him, he stated the obvious. "It's a long walk."

"I know." Mac raked a hand through his hair, aware that people nearby were ignoring them too pointedly. "I guess she has a right to be angry. I caused a scene, didn't I?"

"You did a good job."

"Do we just let her go?"

"Like we agreed, Mac, it's a long walk."

"So which one of us goes after her? I mean, she is your date, and I did intrude."

Lincoln leaned back in his chair, his arms folded. "Usually, I bring a date, I take her home," he drawled in his laconic fashion. "But since she's your wife and you started this, and because convincing the lady she shouldn't go home alone is going to be a little like walking into the den of a lioness who's a mite perturbed, I think I'll reserve that honor for you."

Mac grinned, not at all taken in by Lincoln's smooth withdrawal. "Thanks." He offered his hand. "If I survive, I'll put in a good word for you."

"For me?"

At the doctor's quizzical look Mac laughed. "Yeah, for you. You have to face her tomorrow, remember?"

"So I do." Lincoln's handshake was firm. "Good luck, and don't forget the good word."

"By the way, I've seen you play pro ball. I like your style off the court almost as much as I did on."

"Now it's my turn to say thanks. But there's more at stake than a basketball game. If you didn't have a prior claim on the lady's affections, you wouldn't get by so easily."

"I know. As I said, I like your style." With the wave of a hand, Mac went to catch a lioness.

"Jennifer!"

She paused at the door of a cab that had discharged its passengers. The driver, accustomed to hanging about hoping to pick up a fare for the return trip, was as delighted with the sight of Jennifer as she was with him. She'd wanted to be on her way before Lincoln or Mac decided to come after her. One scene was enough for the evening. She would deal with this quickly.

"Start your meter, driver. I'll be with you shortly." Stepping away from the cab, she turned to face Mac.

He halted before her. In the flash of neon, she was stiff and unnatural, the garish light leeching away every line and expression. Any trace of her anger was hidden. He wanted to touch her, but was sure she'd only wrench away as she had before. "I'm sorry."

"Are you?" In the distance the strident boom of the jukebox was muffled to an indistinct growl. Only an occasional run of notes or a burst of laughter was recognizable. One, Jennifer was certain, was Tiny's, another Sally's. They'd witnessed the incident. "Did it please you to make a spectacle of us in front of the people we both work with? The hospital has been speculating about us for weeks. I hoped it would die for lack of fuel, but you made sure it wouldn't."

"Sweetheart." The endearment spilled out from some subconscious level. "Nobody's speculating about us. They don't have to. Tiny's seen to that. He doesn't mean any harm, but he just can't keep his mouth shut." At her doubting look, he offered proof. "How do you think Avery knew? We haven't met before, and he wasn't certain who I was at first, but it didn't take him long to come to the right conclusions."

"That excuses your behavior? Mac, you acted as if I belong to you. You've not been a part of my life for years, then suddenly, there you are, acting like a jealous husband."

"I am your husband."

"Only technically. You had no right to behave as you did."

"I was out of line. I know it. I'm sorry."

Jennifer lifted her hand, her fingers extended as if she would ward him off. "You've apologized. Let this be the end of it."

"Jennifer." He took a step nearer, gathering her hands in his, drawing them to his chest.

"No!" Slowly, deliberately, she pulled her hands from his grasp and, with that act, seemed to collapse within herself. The determined strength, even her anger, withered away. Burying her face in her hands, she pressed at her temples as if her head ached. Mac was on the verge of reaching for her again, of risking another rejection when she lifted her face from her hands. "I can't do this anymore, Mac." He heard despair and sorrow in her words. "There are things you don't know, things you should know. But I can't deal with them. Not now."

Her eyes were unnaturally bright. In the distortions of neon, he knew the brightness was tears that would not fall. He'd expected recriminations, but was unprepared for this. He had to stand, watching and listening to a soul in agony, and couldn't offer comfort.

That was his punishment. For every known sin, and for the unknown.

"What can I do?" He'd never felt so helpless.

"There's nothing anyone can do." She was trying to be strong. To be as honest as she could. She owed him that, but she couldn't deal with it, not yet. "I can't." She made a futile gesture and backed away. "I'm sorry, Mac."

The look in her eyes pleaded with him to understand all she hadn't said. What she couldn't say.

"I can't," she whispered once more as she climbed into the cab.

Before she could reach for the door, Mac was there, closing it for her. His hand rested for a moment over hers. There was nothing he could say. After a moment he stepped back, giving the cabbie Jennifer's address.

Taillights winked in the darkness, then disappeared before he went to his own car. He sat beneath the steering wheel, uncertain what he should do next. Then he realized there was nothing he could do until Jennifer herself helped him understand.

His drive to his quarters was slow and preoccupied as he wondered what it was he needed so desperately to understand.

"You've had no success at all?" Jennifer laid her pen down on her desk and met Lincoln's bleak look. "Nothing?"

"Not a peep. The kid won't talk, except to say he won't have surgery. It's up to his parents and his surgeon now."

Jennifer spun her chair around. By the calendar March had arrived. The month of spring. The month of despair. A gray sky beyond her window was a reflection of her mood.

"Because we couldn't reach him. Because *I* couldn't reach him," she corrected. Jason was her patient. Lincoln had only stepped in to heal the breach she'd caused. "A tragic decision for his parents. All the more tragic because they must force it on their child."

"Hey!" Lincoln left his seat and went to her, standing behind her chair, watching the same gray sky she watched. He spoke as he would to his young patients. "There was never any decision. Only window dressing for the boy. Whether we reached him or not, the outcome was going to be the same."

"Not quite."

Lincoln wouldn't argue. She wouldn't listen, anyway. Jennifer had been in a strange mood for days. She'd been gradually withdrawing, from him, from everyone but her patients.

"When is surgery scheduled?"

Lincoln bit back a sigh. She intended to have the last painful detail. "Tomorrow at eight."

"It isn't fair, is it, Lincoln?"

"It never has been, it never will be, and there's nothing you can do to change it." He wished he could pick up the telephone and call Mac to take her home. But he dared not. Mac hadn't been visible for days, and his name hadn't crossed her lips. Another part of her withdrawal? "Let me take you home. There's nothing more you can do here today."

"Thanks, but no thanks. I have my car."

"But you will go home?"

"Yes." She was speaking in an absent mutter, her mind on a child she couldn't help. "I think I will go home now."

She was sitting in her kitchen, a cup of tea in her hand and a half-eaten sandwich at her elbow, when the telephone rang.

"Jennifer!" Lincoln began before she had time to speak. "We've trouble here."

"Jason!" The name came instinctively.

"He's on a sixth-floor ledge." Lincoln paused. "He's going to jump."

"Dear heaven!" Jennifer sat heavily on the arm of a sofa. This was what she'd been afraid of, and she'd walked away from this terror-stricken child. "I'm on my way."

The telephone clattered to the floor as she raced for her jacket and keys. The night was crisp and dry. Thank God, rush hour was long over. Even the traffic lights were with her. She didn't spare any thought to what she would have done had they not been. In record time, she was braking in a No Parking zone by the hospital.

The tableau that greeted her was like a scene from a bad melodrama. An assault to her senses, a wrench of her heart, a cold dread in her soul. Police and media vehicles peppered the lawn. Men and women in uniform, in street clothes, in hospital whites, milled in the illuminated night. And pinioned in the glare of spotlights that rose from each side of the lawn to the sixth-floor ledge, stood Jason Keller.

As she flipped her credentials before a fresh-faced cop, Lincoln appeared at her side. Taking her arm, he led her past the cordon, beyond a small command post.

"How long has he been there?" she asked, staring into the bright light.

"Five, maybe ten minutes before I called you."

"What triggered it?"

"The surgery."

"Lincoln—" her fists clenched at her sides, her voice quavered "—why couldn't I help him?"

"None of us could."

"Someone has to go after him."

"Can't. The ledge is too narrow. A catwalk between Jason and the nearest window is impassable. No one can understand how he made it. One man tried. No go. At least he got a microphone close enough that we can hear the boy. An inflatable mattress sort of thing is on the way. A last resort and, I'm afraid, the only one."

"There's nothing else?" she asked in a guilt stricken whisper.

"Nothing I can think of." Drawing her into his arms, he held her, patting her back awkwardly. "Jason rejected you because you hadn't been an athlete. I spent my life on a basketball court. Scholarships paid my college tuition. A pro contract financed the rest. Yet he barely tolerated me. I'm afraid the sight of either of us would put him over the edge.

"But it really had nothing to do with either of us," he said, trying to reassure her. Word had traveled fast. As he held her, Lincoln was watching Mac and Tiny work their way through the crowd. How they'd gotten past the cordon was a mystery, but not a surprise. "I suspect that if Jason had met, say, Mac or Tiny," Lincoln mused, "he would've rejected one for being left-handed, the other for being so big."

As he finished speaking Mac was there. In response to the worried look on his weathered face, Lincoln nodded assurance that Jennifer was all right. Then, faced with the blazing possessiveness in the midnight eyes, he stepped away.

"Jennifer." Mac's voice was hoarse, fear for her giving it a raw edge. A hand on her shoulder turned her to him and, as she came willing into his arms, he sighed and held her close. "I'm sorry, sweetheart." He stroked her hair, hardly aware that it was flying free over her shoulders. "I know how much you wanted to help this boy."

"Someone has to." She raised dry, bleak eyes to his. "Someone must."

"All right." He touched her cheek with the back of his left hand. The bandage had long been discarded, the scratches only fading scars. "I'll try."

"No!" she clutched at him. "Lincoln said . . ."

"Mac, I don't think . . ." Tiny spoke in concert with her, but never finished. He didn't get the chance.

"Tiny!" The change in Jennifer was extraordinary. Her head came up, her gaze finding the big man's. "You did this." She brushed Mac's arms away, turning her fury on a bewildered Tiny. "You with your silly, dangerous games. You put the idea in Jason's head. If he dies you'll be responsible."

Tiny paled beneath the burn of the sun and wind. His kindly eyes were stricken and wounded, his big chest heaved. He looked to the ledge, finding the boy. There was an infinite sadness in him when he looked again into Jennifer's accusing stare. "If I'm to blame, then I should be the one to get him down, not Mac."

"You can't," Mac cautioned. "The ledge is too narrow."

"Sure I can." A grin creased the foreman's homely features. "You just take care of the doc. I'll have the boy down before you know it."

"Tiny." Sally, who was half a step back, caught his wrist. "Be careful."

"Sure I will, darlin'." He dropped a quick kiss on her mouth and shouldered through the crowd.

"Tiny!" Jennifer followed in his wake as Sally had. Kindness that transformed an ugly face into a beautiful face looked down at her. "I didn't mean what I said."

"I know you didn't, Doc."

"Then why are you going?"

"Because I'm the logical one." He patted her hand as it lay on his arm. "After all, it's what I do best."

Jennifer couldn't deny the skill she'd seen. "You'll be careful?"

"Always." He grinned and moved away.

As she watched Tiny speak with a group of uniformed men and women, then disappear through the entrance of the hospital, Jennifer felt Mac at her back, his arms closing about her again. She wanted to sink into the protective circle of his embrace, to hide from the reality of life or death. As afraid as she was to watch, she was more afraid to look away.

In silence, with her back against Mac's chest and the beat of his heart measuring the pain-filled seconds of waiting, she watched as Tiny stepped from a sixth-floor window to the narrow ledge beneath it.

She had to watch, but she was grateful beyond measure for Mac, for Mac's strength as Tiny skimmed over a narrow projection little more than thin air. The catwalk that defeated the first attempt was no deterrent for the man who seemed to fly rather than walk. Incredibly, in a corner only a yard from the cowering boy, Tiny stopped. To a murmur of surprise rising from the ground, he found purchase for his bulky body and settled down.

"What's he doing?" Jennifer demanded. "Why doesn't he go on?"

"Shh," Mac soothed her. "Tiny's giving the boy a way out, letting him make the choice."

"Make the choice!" She was frantic now. Mac held her closer.

"He won't jump, sweetheart. Tiny won't let him. But first he's going to give him the chance to choose to live."

Gripping Mac's arms, feeling the power of his embrace over her breasts and against her pounding heart, she realized through her fear for the boy it was the right way. A way to save not just his body and his life, but his mind and his future.

"Is there enough time? Tiny's willing himself to balance on nothing. How long before even he can't hold on?" Jennifer was sick with what she'd said. "If he falls, it will be my fault. I drove him to this with guilt."

"He won't fall." Sally was by Jennifer's side, her gaze never leaving Tiny. "It isn't your fault. Tiny has no reason to feel guilty—he hasn't danced on the steel since you asked him to stop." Sally risked a look at Jennifer. "Not since before Jason was admitted to the hospital."

Jennifer reeled in Mac's embrace, her accusations thundering in her ears. "Then I sent Tiny into danger." She was shaking. "I'll be to blame."

"You didn't send Tiny, Jennifer," Mac murmured against her cheek. "He went because he wanted to go. Because he cares."

With a squeal of static the microphone on the ledge began an intermittent transmission of the gentle voice of a man and the frightened cries of a child.

"The trick is to live." Tiny's voice was soothing, conversational.

"What do you know?" Jason's reply was muffled, disembodied.

"Not much. Just that any wuss can take a dive." Jason's reply was unintelligible, but Tiny was unperturbed by it. "Taking a dive's easy for the swan. It's the people he leaves behind that hurt."

"I'm not a coward!" Jason's cry reverberated again and again over the crowded lawn.

"Nope. At least not till now."

"You don't know."

"Neither do you, son. You're checking out without finding out. Remember, the trick is to live, making the best of the cards we're dealt. The coward cashes in at the first sign of a bluff."

Jason was crying now. The rest of the exchange was lost in squeals and grunts of static. Jennifer never took her eyes from them, as if by concentrating she could divine what was said. As if by the sheer power of her will, she could keep Tiny from falling and make Jason respond.

For ten more minutes Tiny balanced on a ledge never meant for a man his size. With each passing second, Jennifer sank deeper into despair. She was on the verge of panic, her nails scoring the newly healed flesh of Mac's hand. Then she saw Tiny lift his own hamlike hand, fingers curled and waiting. After a breathless eternity Jason reached out, his fingers brushing, convulsing, clinging to Tiny's.

Jennifer swayed on her feet. Were it not for Mac's arms, she would have fallen. But strength and independence had ceased to matter. As she crumpled against him, all that counted was that Jason Keller had chosen to live.

Eight

—

Another dawn had come and a day had grown old before Jennifer stirred in Mac's arms. He'd laid his watch aside long ago, but by the light beyond her bedroom window he reckoned that afternoon had given way to evening. For hours he'd lain, shoulders braced against an assortment of pillows, her lithe body twined with his, watching as winter's pale gray sky grew darker with time and the threat of rain.

Jennifer had slept long and deeply, and at last, peacefully. Torpor had come quickly in the night, but not peace. She'd tumbled endlessly, writhing body exhausted, mind tormented. So restless that in the stark hours before dawn, Mac considered giving her the sedative Lincoln Avery had quietly tucked in his hand even as she refused it.

In the confusion following Jason Keller's descent from his suicidal perch, none had been calmer than Jennifer. None more professional, nor more gentle with the hurting child. The boy had weighed heavily on her mind for days. Thanks to Tiny's gruff, gloves-off translation of courage, her own late-night session with him had been positive.

The feverish exhilaration of the long-awaited success consumed the little energy she had left. In the shadows beneath it lurked the ever present melancholy. She was tired. They were all tired, and without sleep. But Jennifer's melancholy reached deeper, at a greater cost.

Even the obtuse saw the toll the night had taken. But Jennifer rebuffed concern. Any who dared voice their worry were reassured decisively that she would rest now, and sleep.

And sleep she had, a thrashing, muttering comatose unconsciousness he could not bear.

She hadn't wanted him with her, insisting that all she needed to put the unsettling night behind her was the solitude of her home. Even Lincoln's admission that he would need time to resolve Jason's drama did not sway her. As adamant and immutable as she was, her protests fell on deaf ears. Mac remained more adamant, more immutable.

She would not be alone. No argument dissuaded him, for he had held her through the tense hour and felt the deep, convulsive tremors rack her. He more than any knew she was a reed caught in a torrent of fear and hope. A reed bending when others, who thought themselves stronger, would have broken.

Gracefully, if not willingly, she'd conceded at last, simply to be done with the debate. With his arm about her, he'd led her from the hospital to her car. She'd kept silent through the drive home, as she moved mechanically through her nightly rituals and while he sat beside her bed in the darkness. Then she could fight no longer. In sleep her silence was broken.

Then he sat, watching, listening to the broken rambling of a soul in anguish, until he could stand no more. Until he knew he must touch her and comfort her. Tossing aside a book he couldn't name, he'd stripped off his shirt, his boots and his jeans with their buttons, brads and zippers that would bruise or chafe. Naked, except for the narrow strip of his briefs, he'd lain in the shambles of her bed and taken her in his arms.

With his first touch, she'd grown quiet. The names she'd called, children's names, faded to whispers, and then away. She was a docile child soothed from a nightmare without waking. And she curled against him, seeking in sleep the comfort she would not accept when waking.

Mac held her through the night and into the day, putting aside passion and lust.

Then she moved, her lashes fluttering gold over her cheeks, her body sliding silk against his, and he remembered every lustful desire with inescapable clarity. Carefully disengaging himself, he slipped from her bed. A glance assured that her stirring was only a precursor of true awakening. Gathering his jeans from the floor, stripping off his briefs, he went first to a cold shower, then to her kitchen to make coffee.

With the fragrance of a fine Colombian blend drifting behind him, he returned to her, wearing only jeans. He was damp, refreshed, but his cold shower had done nothing to slake a thirst that had little to do with drink. With passion barely in check, he stood by a door more glass than wood, and with the murky light at his back, he watched her awaken. He suspected she would normally awaken instantly, with body and mind revved to full speed. Today was an exceptional circumstance. Every degree of consciousness gained was languid, every move beguiling.

Tousled and flushed, she surfaced from her slumber like a swimmer leaving the murky depths of a warm, tranquil sea to climb to the sun. Mac hardly breathed. He waited for that first unguarded look of recognition, for the moment she realized she'd slept the day away in his arms.

"Mac?" A whispery tone. She hadn't broken the surface, hadn't quite returned to the real world. Her voice was soft. Her mouth. Her eyes. Everything about her was soft, inviting. "You're still here."

Her voice reached out, surrounding him. "Where else should I be?"

"Sometimes I forget." She shook her head as if amazed at herself. "This is the second time I thought I'd imagined you."

"I'm real, Jennifer." He wanted to show her how very real he was. Served well, for once, by his stubborn Scottish honor, he kept a safe distance.

"I know." Again a nearly silent, silvery whisper that could mean anything. Or perhaps nothing.

Still waking, sweet vulnerable inch by sweet vulnerable inch, Jennifer didn't comprehend what she had done to him. What she was doing to him. With a lazy yawn, brushing her disheveled hair from her face, she leaned on an elbow, not bothering with the neckline of her shirt as it slipped from one shoulder. Her eyelids were heavy, her eyes not quite focused. The veneer of aloof poise she wore to face the world had slipped away in the night.

God help him, she *was* vulnerable. A warm, touchable woman. And he wondered if she could ever be lovelier.

Unconsciously, he drew a long, unguarded breath as revealing as the expression on his face. The effect on Jennifer was as powerful as a thunderbolt. She was instantly aware, sensing his mood.

In the charged atmosphere she was disconcerted by the rumpled bed, the late hour, that he was barefoot and wore no shirt. One startled glance at the heap of pillows at her side, with the unmistakable imprint of his head and shoulders, told a story better than words. But what story? She stared at him, her question in her eyes.

"You were restless, and I held you, Jennifer—" his careful tone was casual "—to quiet your dreams."

"I don't remember my dreams," Jennifer murmured, looking away. "I never do. If they were so terrible, perhaps I should be grateful to you for rescuing me." Feeling his gaze on the swell of her breast bared by the slipping edge of her shirt, she gathered the bright cloth tightly about her neck. "I should thank you for..."

She went utterly still, looking at him now with anxiety leaping into her face as the night came flooding back. "Jason!"

"Jason is better than he's been in a long time. He's found a common bond with Lincoln." At her bewildered look he explained, "I called a while ago from the kitchen."

"Then I have even more to thank you for." Her dismay at their compromising situation was forgotten in other concerns. "Poor Mac, forever to my rescue. You must wonder how I survived over the years."

"Not poor Mac, but hardly Sir Galahad, either." Half turning, he looked out over her back lawn to the park and the lonely secluded trails that were her solace. He remembered her courage, her strength, a daily circumstance, but never more evident than in the long, grueling hours of the traumatic night.

When she was spent, and scared out of her mind for Jason Keller, she tapped that last reserve and was a kind and caring friend, as well as his counselor.

"I don't wonder *how* you survived, Jennifer." He faced her, the light turning him to a somber silhouette. She couldn't read the expression on his shadowed face. The tone and inflection of his words warned her of the direction of his thoughts half a beat too late. "What I wonder," he continued almost gently, "is *what* you survived."

The last, tarrying dregs of sleep vanished. If a blush could heat the skin, the blanching of all its color was frigid. Jennifer felt the cold now. Before she could reply, he was moving closer. With his fingertips he brushed her hair from her face.

"But you did survive—that's what counts." With a tug at the charmingly tangled mane, he grinned. "And now you must be starving. While you grab a shower, I'll see what I can scavenge from the kitchen for brunch."

"Brunch?" Jennifer was struggling for equilibrium, trying to keep pace with his changing moods. "In the evening?"

"Why not in the evening? We'll celebrate Jason's progress."

Heat rose up around her, reached into her, became part of her. It was her breath. The beat of her heart. The rush of her blood. As the healing warmth sought out the cold, a sensual languor washed over her, a lazy tide that swept worries of the night away in its ebb. The gentle spray of the shower caressed her, each drop soothed her. Reminding of another touch that was gentle, that soothed and caressed.

With her face upturned, water pouring over her like summer rain, she let her mind drift to Mac.

When she needed someone, with the onset of the migraine, in the park and with Jason, Mac was with her every step of the way. It hadn't mattered that she'd rebuffed him, or been aloof and cold. When there was trouble, she'd only to turn and he was there, calmly lending his strength. And through it all he'd been kind, kinder than anyone in a long, long time. Kinder than anyone in her life.

He was drawn to her. He'd said it and shown it, time and again. He made no secret of it. He made no promises. Between them there would be no covenant. No ties. Only kindness and desire.

Was it enough?

The answer she needed was as elusive as the steamy mist enveloping her as she stepped from the shower. A tender dilemma that was frightening and exhilarating at once. Like the mist, its mystery was all around her. Like the mist, there was no escaping it.

"He wants me."

Jennifer bowed her head, her hands clutched beneath her chin. Standing naked, water sliding unnoticed in glittering streams down her body, she faced the truth.

"And I want him."

At last she'd said the words that had lain in the back of her thoughts from the moment he'd come back into her life. Not even fear and grief could change the truth. Desire had become a living thing, a constant, when their lives touched.

In the absence of love, for only one night, would kindness be enough?

Yes.

Her hand was shaking, but this time not from alarm, when she took a thick terry robe from a hook by the door. There were things Mac didn't know. That he could never in a lifetime understand or forgive. But soon his responsibilities at the building site would be discharged, and he would be on his way to the next site. She would be of no more concern than she'd been before. Then perhaps secrets that would only cause suffering could remain secret, after all.

This was only an interlude. A moment in time that had never been and would never come again. Another time, another place.

There was kindness.
And there was desire.

The table was set. Napkins were folded, the silver perfectly aligned. The fragrance of fresh-brewed coffee blended with the scent of toasted bread. Mac was dressed now and absorbed again in the low-lying evergreens fringing the park.

"They make you think of home, don't they?" Jennifer asked from the doorway.

He swung about, his expression neutral.

"The evergreens," she explained. "They make you think of home."

Mac smiled. His thoughts were much closer than North Carolina. They were with a woman who walked beneath the moon and was lovely in its light. Almost as lovely as she was now. "We always seemed to smell of them," he murmured as he drank in the sight of her. His voice was husky and he had no idea what he was saying as he rambled on. "No matter how hard we scrubbed, their scent was still there. Sharp, stringent."

"Pleasant," Jennifer added to his list.

"I suppose it was." He smiled again and dragged his thoughts from the fascinating journey of a droplet of water as it disappeared into the hidden cleft of her breasts. He was tempted to take her in his arms and with his lips discover the path the darkly glittering drop had taken. But the meal he'd made was waiting, and Jennifer needed sustenance, not his lust. "Come." He gestured her to the table. "You've been without food nearly twenty-four hours."

Jennifer crossed the room to him. Taking the chair he held for her, she waited until he was seated across from her. "This looks wonderful. I didn't realize you were so handy in the kitchen."

"I've become a passable cook over the years. So long as the fare needn't be more than filling."

Over the years. A phrase with a lonely ring. What had his life been like? How alone? For months on end he was cut off from his family, his country, living in primitive conditions. His only tastes of civilization came on short junkets to the cities. And in the rarer and shorter visits home.

At his first mention of food, she'd been famished. Thoughts of the utter loneliness of a man away from the family he loved crowded in and her appetite disappeared. Ignoring her filled plate, she folded her hands inside the wide sleeves of her robe. Her fingers gripped her wrists, her nails piercing half-moons in her flesh.

Had she done this to him? Had she set him adrift from everything he loved?

"Mac." His name in the silence was a startling, unexpected sound. When she looked up she found him watching her, his food as unwanted as her own. Beneath the keen indigo stare, she couldn't find the words to ask what she must. Admitting defeat, she settled for one word that asked it all. One. "Why?"

Why hadn't he dissolved the marriage when she hadn't? Why hadn't he found someone else to love? Why had he stayed in South America so long and why had he finally come back to his own country? But more than anything, why was he here, now, in her home? Why did he want her?

The unspoken questions lay between them, as intangible as the fragrance of coffee. And as unmistakable.

Mac picked up a fork, then laid it down again, tracing the pattern on its stem with a fingertip. Jennifer was afraid he didn't intend to answer, until he began to speak in a distant voice, as if he spoke of things rarely addressed.

"When I left, I wanted to get as far away as possible. So far you could never hurt me again." With a wince he corrected himself. "So far we couldn't hurt each other."

"I called you before you left for South America," Jennifer ventured in a taut, guarded voice. "There were things we needed to discuss."

"I didn't take your calls because I couldn't, Jennifer. If I'd heard your voice, I would've trashed the little pride I had left and accepted your terms. We would've gone back to the privileged life I couldn't afford. The country club, the cars, the parties, the evenings at Madame Zara's. In the end, I would've been forced to take the position your father offered."

"Madame Zara." Jennifer mused over happier times. "She loved the McLachlan clan as much as her own family.

She was happiest when one of you was in Atlanta and dined with her. Especially you, her bonny Gemini."

"That didn't change the fact that I couldn't afford the time or the cost of reserving a nightly table in her restaurant."

"I understand that now. I understand a lot of things I didn't before." Her smile was a grimace. "I left you no option but to leave."

"I didn't have to run."

"I think you did, or my father and I would have destroyed you."

Mac did not hear the self-condemnation. Once begun, his memories would not stop. "I waited for months for that flimsy bit of paper that would be the end of what we'd had. When it didn't come, I assumed it was lost, that I was the last to know. I read every newspaper from home to the last page, half expecting a story of the social event of the year. The wedding you never had with me."

"It was the same for me." Jennifer relived the anguish of searching through each day's mail and newspapers, and the relief coupled with a curious regret when there were no stiff white envelopes containing papers with the names of a strange law firm emblazoned across them. She recalled the times she'd prayed she would find something in her mail or read an announcement in the paper. Then, at least, the waiting would end.

He'd lived the same uncertainty, but she took no pleasure in it. Instead, she wanted to touch him, to brush away the frown that scored his handsome face and comfort him as he'd comforted her through the night. Her nails burrowed deeper into the soft inner side of her wrists as she suppressed the urge. "I always thought that when I didn't initiate the divorce, you would do it. I was constantly expecting to hear that you'd found someone and wanted your freedom."

Mac pushed his plate away. He still didn't look at Jennifer. "At first I was too angry for a new relationship. Unjust as it was, my anger was directed at all women, not just you. Then there was no time. Then no opportunity. Finally, entanglements of any sort weren't important. My commitment was to my work. It consumed me, became my mistress.

"Ultimately, that was the reason I left South America." He lifted his gaze to hers. "I didn't like the man I had become. A cold, bitter bastard who had no thought or time for anything but his work."

"So you came home to end a farce of a marriage and build a normal life." Jennifer had no claims on him. She'd forfeited them a lifetime ago, yet it hurt to imagine Mac with a wife and a family.

A little girl with eyes as blue as her father's.

Pain clawed at the back of her throat. "You've been in the country six months." Her voice was hollow with old grief. "What have you been doing?"

Mac clasped his hands on the table. His knuckles were white against his weather-stained skin. "I wanted to spend a few weeks with my brothers and their families. The rest I needed to establish the business."

"Now that your life's in order again, you'll want the divorce." Now that it was real, not presumption, the word was ugly, a legal declaration of failure. A ridiculous sentiment, for she'd failed Mac and their marriage long ago.

"I don't have a timetable, but we should resolve the issue of our divorce."

Jennifer couldn't speak. Silence was a chasm between them.

Mac's fingers untangled, one hand lay fisted on the table, the other raked brutally through his hair. The stifling hush was pervasive, painful. He wanted done with it. "I should leave you to what's left of your evening."

"No." She reached across the chasm, her hand closing about his wrist as he rose.

"You've had a rough time, Jennifer. Maybe I was wrong. Maybe time alone is what you need."

She dismissed his reversal. She couldn't think of what was right or wrong now. "You haven't answered my question."

His voice was as level as his look. "I gave you what answers I could."

"Except the most important." Her hair had begun to dry, and it spilled down the back of her bulky robe as she looked up at him. Her hand was still on his wrist. "You haven't told me why you're here."

"Don't." His chest heaved in a deeply drawn breath. His eyes closed to shield himself from her. "You don't know what you're asking."

"I've asked before. If I didn't know then what I was asking, I know now."

"Dammit, Jennifer."

"Tell me why you're here." Her hold did not waver, nor her resolve. "Tell me what you want."

"Dammit!" he cursed again, and this time his drawn breath shuddered through him. "You mean to have it, don't you? Every gut wrenching word!"

He pulled away from her grasp, slowly, deliberately. Jennifer made no effort to keep him. She didn't speak or look away as he towered over her.

"I'm here because I can't help myself. Because I can't stay away." His blue gaze was nearly black. "I want Jennifer McLachlan, body and soul. Why? For how long? God only knows. You've heard it before, like a broken record." His voice was bleak, strained. He sighed almost wearily. "I won't bore you with it anymore."

He touched her cheek, letting his fingers trail over the curve of her jaw to her throat before falling away. "For what it's worth," he murmured, his anger quieted as suddenly as it had come, "you're a hell of a woman, Jennifer McLachlan. There isn't a man among us who would begrudge you that name."

He'd spun away without ceremony and was halfway across the kitchen, striding to the door, when she stopped him with words more powerful than a steel trap. "Please, don't go."

He paused, shoulders back, head half-turned, eyes screwed shut in a wincing scowl. Tension rippled through him. She could see it in the angle of his chin, in the taut lines of his body. A muscle quivered in his jaw, and beneath the shaggy growth of his hair, tendons in his neck were prominent with his effort to keep still. "I have to go, Jennifer. If I stay, we both know what would happen."

"If you stay you'll make love to me."

The truth, stated bluntly, leaving no room for evasion. "Right or wrong, Jennifer, I'm not sure I could stop myself."

"I hope not."

He couldn't respond. He couldn't find the words. His blood moving with a sultry heat, his thoughts fevered, disoriented, he could only feel.

He didn't know when she left her seat at the table, nor did he hear her steps, but she was near. So near he could smell the mingled scents of soap and shampoo and imagine the rustle of the terry robe as it brushed the arch of her bare feet.

She was naked beneath the robe. Only a bit of bulky turquoise terry hid what he wanted so shockingly.

She touched his arm, her hand small against tense, corded muscles beneath his shirt. "Mac."

His name. A plea.

He was lost.

Turning to her, he caught her roughly to him. Something dark and wild and hungry was unleashed in him. His mouth ground hard against hers. His tongue plunged into her mouth, hot and seeking. She was light for a man too long in darkness. Freedom for desires held too closely. But the wildness would not be tamed, nor the primal hunger so easily sated.

One hand tangled in her hair, the other slid low on her hip, drawing her to him. The heat of their bodies fused, rising in a heady mix of her scent and his. And the hand at her hip drew her closer still.

Jennifer heard a ragged cry. A low sound, beginning deep in a tortured throat. An uncivilized sound, as wild as his passion, as primitive as his hunger. And she knew, dimly, that the throat that uttered it was her own.

She was afraid, and had no idea what it was she feared. She was desperate, and the reason for desperation eluded her. Then, frantic and incoherent, even that little reason escaped her, and she knew only exquisite relief when he tugged her robe from her shoulders.

Sliding it from her, he clutched it in one hand and flung it violently away. For a long, sweet moment he held her from him, his gaze moving over her bare breasts, down the lean curved line of waist and hip and abdomen. And lower to shadowed gold.

"God help us both," he muttered, tearing his gaze with effort from that secret part of her. His eyes rose to hers. Blue fire burned in them, the fire of desire. Then his hands were on her. Framing her face for another kiss, and another. Sliding through her hair to her shoulders. Skimming down the slope of her breasts. Holding them, sliding beneath them, taking their weight in his palms. Teasing the soft areolas with his fingertips, he bent to take first one hard, tiny peak in his mouth, then the other.

Jennifer gasped. Her head was thrown back. Her hands were buried in his hair, holding him, trembling as his suckling sent new and devastating sensations streaming through her. Flashes of pleasure so powerfully sensual they bordered on pain seared a path from breasts to loins. Each suckling tug at a nipple set her shivering as the gathering anxiety of ecstasy and torment became too much.

"No more. I can't stand any more." She clung to him, her eyes closed, her body cleaving to his. "Oh, Mac!" Her hair swirled wildly about her shoulders as her head moved in denial. "I can't."

Jennifer had no idea what she said or what she did. Something wonderful and frightening deep inside her wouldn't be still. Like a storm, it grew, vital, intense, threatening to consume her.

"I know," Mac murmured. Lifting his mouth to hers, he kissed her, this time gently. Cradling her head in his palms, he soothed her panic, banking the fires of passion before they burned too soon out of control. "I know, love. I know. Some things are too wonderful to bear. But we've only begun, and the most wonderful is waiting. The miracle of loving is almost ours." Crooning his half-whispered chant, he swept her from her feet and took her in his arms to her bed.

Jennifer had no time to be amazed at his strength, or the power of legs that could sustain them when hers would not. She had no time to marvel that the covers of her bed had been smoothed back. Or to question when his jeans and shirt had been tossed aside.

There was only time to open her arms to him, and then the passion banked ever so newly by his moment of tenderness became a holocaust.

This time there was no panic. When the ardor of his touch careered to a mind-rending pitch, she went with it, accepted it. Mind, body, heart and soul.

She felt the delicious crush of his body, the granite muscles of his belly pressing against her, the urgency of his desire. The hotter his passions burned, the gentler his touch. With maddening expertise he stroked her and caressed her, discovering exquisitely sensitive places not even Jennifer knew, awaking with subtle mastery erotic responses. With the sweep of his fingertips he blazed a trail of fire over her body. With his mouth and tongue he followed, and the fire burned still hotter. Body taut and quivering with each new delight, Jennifer wondered what more she could survive.

With his body as taut as hers, his wonder as great, Mac took her with him to the brink where the heart seemed to stop, and the mind. Where there was only sensation and each more wonder-filled and devastating than the last. When passions threatened to brim over, he found himself wanting to prolong the excitement, the sweet agony. He wanted the final ecstasy, but first he was tempted to steal another honeyed kiss. To nibble again at an earlobe. To suckle one perfect nipple as her breast rose in her breathless response to his caress.

His kisses ranged over her body. From knee to hip, to skim over the contracting muscles of her stomach. From the hollow of her navel to the hollow of her throat, his tongue dipping into them, touching the pulse that throbbed with the vigor of her racing heart. Her body gleamed with the moist flush of excitement, droplets like morning dew, that tasted of salt and nectar. In the failing light, the glow of a lamp spilled over her, and each delicate curve became shimmering silk, each sweet shadow a mystery.

And as the day grew darker, his hands glided over her, discovering again and again the mysteries, reveling in their secret sweetness. Savoring the miracle of what his touch could do.

Until, at last, with a muffled cry she drew him to her.

Her hands were in his hair, her mouth on his. Beneath him her body writhed to be closer. Passion so carefully dammed within him swept over the floodgates. Flood or conflagration, there was no taming it. More than ever in his life, he wanted to be gentle. But all the gentleness in him had been expended in his slow, sweet seduction. There was a ruthlessness in what he felt, a reckless need he feared would hurt her. Then came the final realization that he'd nothing to protect her. From himself, from the consequences of their mating.

He tore his mouth from hers, his head came up. Weight borne on trembling hands, he reared over her, his eyes blazing down. There was a brief moment when he might have regained his sanity. A moment when a single sign of fear from Jennifer would have stopped him. But Jennifer didn't stop him, and he saw that she wasn't afraid.

And rising up to meet the culmination of his passion, her body opening to his with abandon, she proved the last thing she wanted was gentleness and patience.

Filled with the wonder of lost pleasure, filled with him, Jennifer gave herself up to the ruthlessness. Meeting fury with fury of her own, she rode the crest, higher and higher, her body in concert with his. Until that special moment when the world stopped. Until the gathering twilight was shattered by her wild, shuddering cry. Until her cry was echoed in a deeper note by Mac.

In one instant of exquisite clarity, she knew this was her desperation. And that fear had been need, instead.

Then all the wonders that had gone before became one and the miracle was hers.

Sometime in the night, in an hour too dark to judge, Mac awoke. No sound had stirred him. But new trusts are not easy. It was the utter quiet that pierced the sleep of a man accustomed to the jungle. To whom the complete cessation of sound meant trouble. But there was no trouble here, and the night was calm beyond the window.

The storm that had been only a threat had moved on. The air was still, the house quiet. The only motion was the gentle rhythm of Jennifer's breathing.

Her head was on his shoulder, her body tucked into the curve of his, her fingers tangled in the downy pelt that covered his chest. Touching his lips to her brow, he gathered her closer. He was content as he hadn't been in a lifetime.

He'd expected the mind-shattering culmination of passion too long denied. He'd wanted it, even needed it to be free. For ten years he'd been a man alone. There were no holds on him. No fetters from the past, no claims on his future. Then her laughter had drifted through a winter twilight and taken him captive.

She'd drawn him to her at every turn. Jennifer McLachlan, a woman like none he'd ever known. A selfless friend, a compassionate physician, a beautiful mystery.

A lover he must have.

This was to be the final exorcism, and then he would be free. But he hadn't reckoned on the contentment. Nor with the sadness that this would be the last night he would ever hold her.

Lying with her in his arms, he listened to the silence and wondered at his sadness.

When he awoke again it was to the touch of her hand at his cheek. Coming instantly aware, he realized she was no longer in his arms. "Jennifer?"

"Shh." Her hand moved from his cheek to his lips. "Don't say anything. This night is too wonderful to sleep away, or even for talking."

In the little illumination gleaned from a lightening sky, she bent over him. A spirit of the night, with her bare body mesmerizing and her dancing fingers enchanting. When he shivered and caught those maddening hands in his, she tried to pull away.

"No," she whispered. "This time is mine."

She meant to tantalize him, to turn the embers that lay deep inside him to white-hot flame. She wanted to make him cry out her name in a plea. She wanted him to be desperate and afraid, and not understand why. She wanted him to need her, and when the end was near, she wanted him to demand the release only she could give him.

Mac looked into a face too shadowed to read. But her body lying over his was like a wild bird's, hot, thrumming with excitement, aroused. Bringing her hands to his lips, he kissed them and released her. Her sultry, exultant laugh told him all she intended. Even as he gave himself to her teasing seduction, Mac knew she had succeeded before she began.

In the last of the darkness before the dawn, before their night was done, Jennifer made love to the man who was her husband.

To Mac, who wondered how he could ever leave her now.

Nine

Mac's heels were a solid thud in the corridor. His face was bleak, his pace quick as he passed hospital staff and office personnel without a word or a glance. He barely noticed the group he skirted deep in discussion by an open door. Days of watching and wondering, then of worry, had proved the one he was seeking would not be among them.

At the end of the corridor, with the flat of his hand, he pushed through double doors. A few more paces and he halted abruptly at Sally Brown's desk.

"Where is she?" His demand was rough and raw, with an edge of steel.

Ever calm, ever efficient, the secretary looked up from the sheaf of reports she was sorting. For more than a week, she'd watched and worried with Tiny as Mac had gone from too jovial and gregarious to morose and withdrawn. Finally he'd stopped coming to A Cozy Little Place completely. In the time since she'd seen him, he'd grown haggard and thinner.

If she'd spent her evenings steeped in concern for Mac, her days were no different. The first weeks of March were always difficult for Jennifer. No one among the staff knew what personal hell this time was for her, only that it was. Sally speculated now it was a hell they shared.

Laying aside the reports, she answered honestly, "I don't know where Dr. McLachlan is."

"Come off it, Sally. She's not been to the hospital for days. Her car is in her drive and there are lights on in her house, but she hasn't been to the park or answered her telephone. It isn't like Jennifer to go off without giving notice of where she can be reached. So, quit being evasive and tell me where she's gone, and with whom."

"I'm not being evasive, Mac. And you're right, normally Dr. McLachlan wouldn't go off without giving notice of where she'd be. But this isn't a normal time." Sally pursed her lips and frowned. "Then again, maybe it is."

"Don't be cryptic, woman! I haven't the patience for it." A frustrated gesture punctuated his comment. "Are you saying Jennifer's done this before? On a random day she just disappears and no one knows why or where?"

"That's exactly what I'm telling you." Sally had worked too long at this job, dealt too often with anxious parents whose impotence turned to anger, to be ruffled by Mac's derision. "But there's nothing random in it. The time is always mid-March, it's been the same in the three years she's been on staff."

"Why the devil are you giving me this rubbish? If anything Jennifer's too scrupulous. She wouldn't just go off—"

Impervious to his barb, Sally interrupted his harangue. "She doesn't just go off, and she doesn't forget her responsibilities. She begins by seeing to it her patients will be cared for by other staff members. She speaks with the parents, informing them she'll be away for a while. Then one day, she simply isn't here."

Even then Mac couldn't take it in, couldn't make what he was hearing fit the woman he'd come to know. "Not sick leave," he muttered. "No one gets sick on schedule. Then what?" His anger and irritation turned to bewilderment. "A vacation?"

"If it is, it's never a good one. When she comes back she looks worse than you do. If that's possible." A wry look took in his gaunt, unshaven face and sunken eyes.

Mac dismissed the pointed observation. "You couldn't reach her if one of her patients was in crisis?"

"Not even then."

Disbelief died hard. "Jennifer wouldn't do that."

"No, she wouldn't. Not if she could keep from it."

"And because she can't, she just disappears?"

"Exactly." A patient answer for the same question.

Skepticism crumbled, but the haunted look in his eyes didn't change. "What does it mean?"

"Only Jennifer knows the answer to that." Sally abandoned the formal address of the office. She was speaking now of a woman who had become her friend, not her employer.

Mac raked a hand though his already disheveled hair. "When I realized she was gone, I thought it was something I'd done."

"No." Sally shook her head, then added, "At least not lately."

"Not lately? How did you arrive at that conclusion?"

"It's evident, I think, that whatever this fugue is its cause lies in the past." Her uncompromising gaze held his. "You were part of that past."

"What could it be? Dear heaven, what could it be?" Mac was speaking under his breath, more to himself than Sally. His anguish and confusion were nearly palpable. "She was a naive kid and I was a stiff-necked idealist when we met. The marriage lasted six months, then failed because we were incompatible and too young and too stubborn to compromise. It might not have been pretty, but there was nothing disastrous in it."

"Nothing that you know about."

"What!" Mac was disconcerted by her blunt statement.

"Do you know what went on in her life after you left?"

"We didn't keep in touch. I was in South America. She was . . ." He stuttered to a halt, amazed that he didn't know where Jennifer had spent the years before she came to Barclay. Or why. "My God! I don't know. I was too busy coping with my own wounds to consider what she might be going through. I assumed her father would see to it she didn't miss me for longer than a few months." A bitter frown scored his forehead. "I was certain he would."

But Jennifer had quarreled with her father. Edwin Burke hadn't been a part of her life since shortly after their marriage ended. It made no sense. Nothing made any sense. Except that Jennifer had built a life for herself, without her father, without him. With no friends and, he knew now, with no other lovers. Ducking his head, Mac massaged his burning eyes, searching for answers when there were none.

"Mac," Sally said quietly, "why did you come today? Why do you care where Jennifer is or what she's going through?"

He wanted to evade the truth, but Sally's level gaze wouldn't permit it. "I thought I might have hurt her again." And hadn't he? He'd made love to her and with her, then left her for days without a word. And now she'd disappeared. After a long while of dealing with his callousness and his cowardice, he said, "I thought she might need me."

"And if she should?"

"Then I'll do whatever I can for her."

"One more time, Mac. Why do you care?"

This time he couldn't hold that piercing gaze. "I don't know, Sally."

Her cropped head moved from side to side in exasperation. "I never figured any friend of Tiny's for a liar, Mac. But you're lying now. To me, or to yourself. Until you settle that question, believe me, you'll be no help to Jennifer."

A valid point he couldn't refute. "Then I'll have to settle it, won't I?"

Sally studied him a moment longer. "I think maybe you already have. You wouldn't be here if you hadn't."

"Maybe." The response was delivered with a sharp nod, and he turned on his heel and strode away.

"What are you going to do?"

"I'm going to find Jennifer."

The double doors shut with a thump behind him, but not before he heard Sally murmur, "Good luck." Then, "To both of you."

Mac slumped in his seat. His phenomenal ability to sleep had deserted him, and he'd risen from another restless night to take up his post again outside Jennifer's house. Though he still hadn't seen her, the lights inside had been turned off and on too sporadically for automatic timers. On that bit of detection, he'd drawn the conclusion that she was home. He'd spent the better part of a day and most of a night watching from his parking place half a block away. Now another day was beginning. Sooner or later, she would have to leave the house.

If not today, then another. However long it took, he would wait.

He'd settled in for a long, cramped siege under the steering wheel of his car, when the front door of the small house opened and Jennifer emerged. For an instant, his straining eyes didn't register what they were seeing. Only the slam of her car door snapped him from his inertia.

By the time she'd backed out of the driveway, Mac was alert and ready to follow. He'd wrestled with his conscience on the matter of this invasion of her privacy and had finally come to terms with it. This was something he had to do. Some sixth sense told him the answers to all the questions that had plagued him would be answered by the solving of this last mystery.

Giving the distastefulness of what he did no more thought, he followed, keeping a careful distance behind. At first, though she wasn't dressed for it, he assumed she was going to the hospital. But a block short of it, she turned onto a road that eventually led to the interstate traversing most of Georgia.

She kept a steady speed on the highway, never exceeding the limit and rarely dropping below it. Were it not for the very steadiness, this might have been a midmorning ramble. Exit after exit flashed by, and Atlanta and its suburbs were left behind. Mac had begun to think she had no destination, after all, when she turned onto a small, little-used road, and following her unnoticed became a problem.

There was a strong chance that whatever had driven her first to seclusion, then here, was disturbing enough that she wouldn't recognize his car. But it was a chance he couldn't take. Hanging back, keeping her barely in his sight, he trailed her cautiously. In a small village, which was no more than a shop or two and a few houses, she pulled into a drive. Mac waited again a little distance away and was startled when she emerged with a small bouquet of yellow flowers in her arms.

"A florist? Now what is this all about?" he muttered as he engaged the gears and resumed his meandering chase. The day had grown more and more curious, but that was nothing compared to his surprise when she turned one last time onto an unpaved drive leading to a quaint, small chapel.

Mac had gotten too close to remain unobserved, but Jennifer still did not see him as she left her car. Head down, apparently lost in thought, and flowers in hand, she by-passed the chapel to climb a tiny hillock. At its crest, guarded by a low wrought-iron fence, lay a small cluster of graves.

"What on earth, Jennifer?" he asked as he kept his gaze on her retreating back. "Is it your mother?"

Mac searched his memory. Had Jennifer mentioned her mother? He couldn't remember. Mary Burke was always a sickly woman, almost a nonentity, living in the shadow of her powerful husband and, tragically, easily forgotten. Try as he might to remember now, Mac drew a blank.

Had Mary Burke not survived the years he'd been away? Was she the motive for this journey? Had Jennifer come to the little cemetery on the hillside to honor her mother on some special occasion?

Perplexed, he settled down to wait again.

The day was a pleasant one. March was kindly offering a preview of spring, yet a week away. The sun was bright, and the day was cool but comfortable. Reaching into a brief-case on the passenger seat, Mac drew out the preliminary workup of a proposal he would be submitting soon for another project. Throughout what remained of the morning and into the afternoon, he pored over papers, trying to absorb crucial facts. His mind constantly straying to the hillock, its graves and the small figure huddled there.

The sun was dropping and the temperature with it when he stuffed the papers back into his briefcase, finally admitting that all he was seeing was gibberish. Gripping the steering wheel, he stared up at Jennifer. If she'd moved at all, it couldn't be discerned from this distance.

It was getting late. The sun would be gone soon, and the springlike day would revert to winter. Jennifer had worn only a light jacket and slacks. By now she was likely already chilled. The shadow of a lone oak had crept gradually toward her and at last enveloped her in the gloom, and still she hadn't risen.

"Jennifer," Mac muttered, as if by saying her name he could will her to come away from her grief.

But Jennifer did not come away. The sun touched the crest of a distant hill. In a little while there would be only twilight to light her way.

When he'd seen the final destination of her drive, Mac had taken care not to intrude on a troubled time. Now he was seized by the certainty that he was a part of that trouble, and that she needed him. Perhaps as she never had before.

The conviction was so strong he was out of the car and shrugging into his jacket before there was time for second thoughts. Closing the door quietly, he crossed the dusty road and climbed the grassy hill. The gate he opened was old and rusty, and creaked a protest at being disturbed. If Jennifer heard, she didn't react.

Mac weaved through the cluster of graves. Most were old, their stones weathered, the dates he read from another century. The little cemetery had clearly fallen into disuse, except the plot where Jennifer knelt.

There were two stones not yet worn by time and weather. One, as he'd anticipated, was Mary Burke's. The other, with the bouquet of daffodils lying on its marked space, was obscured by Jennifer. Even in the dimming light, Mac was aware that there were drying tears on her lowered face. He took a step closer, wondering who lay beside Mary Burke and why this small grave caused such lasting sorrow.

"Jennifer." He bent to touch her shoulder, but at the sound of his voice her head lifted and the stone was visible. Mac's hand stopped in midmotion, his fingers curling over nothing as he stared at the name and inscription written there.

At first glance he couldn't comprehend what he saw. He shook his head to clear his mind. The breath he'd caught and forgotten leaked from his lungs like a shrinking balloon. As if it would bring them into sharper focus, he read the words aloud in a voice that belonged to a stranger.

"Sarah Hope McLachlan, beloved daughter of Jennifer Burke and ..." He turned a stricken face to Jennifer, certain he'd lost his mind. It couldn't be. Woodenly he turned again to the stone. "Beloved daughter," he read again in a whisper, "of Jennifer Burke and Robert Bruce McLachlan."

He moved another step, his attention riveted on the stone. On the dates marking the pitifully short life of Sarah Hope McLachlan, who died seven years before, on her second birthday.

For a moment all he could think was how obscene it was that a child should die on her birthday. Then the world as he knew it tilted beneath him, and his life would never be the same again.

"My daughter?" Shock mingled with horror as the brutal truth ripped through him. There was agony in his face when he turned again to Jennifer. "My God! My daughter, and I never knew."

"Sarah." There were tears streaming down Jennifer's face anew, but Mac didn't see them.

"She would have been nine today." Somehow the realization made his loss that much greater.

Jennifer rose from her knees. She wanted to put her arms around him and hold him, but the forbidding glitter in his look stopped her.

"Why, Jennifer? Why did you do this? Did you hate me *that* much? So much that you kept her from me?" He was rigid, his fists clenched. A muscle rippled in his jaw. His eyes were blue infernos. "Damn you. Is this your revenge? Did you cheat Sarah of her father to extract your pound of flesh?"

"No, Mac!" She took a step toward him, her hand lifted in entreaty, her own heartache put aside in the face of his. "You're wrong. It wasn't like that."

"Stay away!" He warded her off. "For your own sake, just stay away."

"Mac, you have to listen. You have to understand." Ignoring his warning, she clutched at his sleeve, only to lose her grip as he whirled on her, grasping her shoulders in a brutal hold.

"I was half out of my mind when you disappeared. I thought I'd hurt you again by making love to you, then leaving you." His chest heaved in an uneven breath. "And I couldn't bear the thought that I'd been so cruel." His fingers were talons, bruising her flesh. "But I could take lessons from you in the art of cruelty, couldn't I?"

Jennifer stood in his hard grasp, her shock at seeing him in the secluded little cemetery replaced by the horror of what he believed. "I loved you. I didn't stop loving you just because our marriage didn't work. Because I loved you, I couldn't have done what you've accused me of."

"No?" He released her to kneel by the grave. With his fingertips, he traced the brief record of a brief life. "Then tell me, how do you explain a child I never held? A daughter who died and, God help me, Jennifer, I don't even know why."

Tears gathered in his eyes and spilled down his cheeks unheeded. Their silent fall down his haggard face was her undoing. Risking his anger, she twined her hands in his hair and drew his head to her breasts. He was coiled and tense in her embrace, but didn't move away. As she stroked his hair, murmuring broken phrases of comfort, he suffered her touch, only suffered it. After a moment, defeated by his passive rejection, Jennifer moved away.

"I'm sorry," she stammered. "I shouldn't have done that. I should have realized you don't want anything from me. Least of all comfort."

"You're right, I don't." One daffodil caught the last rays of the dying sun, and he touched it as if to keep its warmth.

"Daffodils were her favorite."

Mac didn't respond. He'd withdrawn to a place beyond anger, a place she couldn't reach. Rising to his feet, he turned his back on her. She no longer existed. "I'll come another day, Sarah. I promise."

Another day, to mourn his daughter alone.

With her heart in her throat, Jennifer watched as he walked among the graves and through the gate.

"Mac."

He didn't turn around.

"You have to listen." She was at the iron fence, her hands closed over it like claws. "I called you. You wouldn't take my calls. I wrote you. My letters came back unopened. I went to Rick's apartment and you were already gone. Then my father convinced me you wanted nothing to do with me or with the child I was carrying."

Mac's pace had been slowing. Now he stopped completely. He turned, looking up at her through the gloom. "Your father?"

"Yes."

"It always came down to that, didn't it, Jennifer? It was always your father or me." His bitterness was like a knife, cutting to the heart.

Mute in her pain, Jennifer watched him go. She watched as he reached his car. She was watching still as taillights blinked over the dusty road, then faded out of sight.

Her father or Mac. And Mac would never know the choice she'd made.

Returning to the tiny grave, she knelt again, remembering the child with eyes like her father's. The child of the man she'd loved.

"And the black cat who was a dog, after all, turned into a turtle."

"I'm sure you're right, Lincoln." Jennifer tapped her pen on Lincoln Avery's desk. Her gaze was skewed a fraction to his left, to the window behind him.

"Which part are you sure is right, Jennifer?" Then to draw her attention back from wherever it had wandered, he raised his voice a startling few decibel. "Which part, Jennifer?"

"Pardon?" Eyes wide in surprise, she turned her glance to him.

Lincoln grinned. "After we discussed Jason's tremendous progress, you drifted away."

"I did?"

"I just told you that a black cat who was really a dog turned into a turtle, and you agreed with me."

"Oh, no." Her face flamed as she laid down her pen, forcing herself to be still.

"Yep." Lincoln's grin faded. "You've been back at the hospital for several days, Jennifer. You've caught up with all that's gone on while you were away, and you're back in the routine. Yet there are times when you act as if there's a curtain between you and the rest of the world. As if you can't quite stay with us."

"I'm sorry, I don't mean to be inattentive."

"No one knows that better than I."

Her attempt at a smile was a distracted grimace, but the sincerity in her voice was unmistakable. "I appreciate your patience."

"I can be more than patient. Why don't you tell me what's bothering you? Perhaps I can help."

"No one can help, Lincoln. I made a mistake a long time ago that changed the course of several lives. Nothing in the world can undo it."

"Mistakes that can't be put right can be overcome if it's important enough."

"Not always."

"But you won't know that until you try. Do you want to try, Jennifer?"

"I don't know."

Lincoln leaned back in his chair, his chin resting on his steepled fingers. "Would this mistake that can't be undone have anything to do with your absence from the hospital?"

"It has everything to do with it."

"Does it involve Mac?"

"Yes."

The curt response didn't surprise him. At least it was progress. "Would you like to talk about it?"

"No!"

She practically bounded from her chair. Arms crossed protectively over her breasts, she began her habitual pacing and discovered that in Lincoln's little office pacing would take her to the window. Since her return to the hospital she'd been drawn to the window at every turn. And at every turn she'd rejected the impulse. Staring out at the shell of a building solved nothing.

She hadn't seen Mac in days. Not since he'd left her standing by their daughter's grave. Where was he? What was he thinking? How could she make him understand?

"Yes." She didn't know she was going to agree until the word was out.

Lincoln's carefully bland gaze never left her as he waited for the rest.

"Yes," she heard herself say again, "I'd like to talk about it. If there's a way I'd like to overcome it."

Her lanky colleague smiled, and his whole body seemed to nod. "I think you've taken the first step toward a recovery that's been a long time coming."

Jennifer was silent. Her arms were still crossed, her body taut. In spite of all her efforts, she stood by the window staring at the men who were leaving the site, their day's work done. Mac was not among them.

Moving away, she tried to concentrate. She'd decided to speak to Lincoln on impulse. Following through was the difficult part. She wasn't aware she'd returned to her seat until she found herself facing him with nothing to say. Her grave laugh was shaky and a little uncertain. "I don't know where to begin."

"There is a beginning, isn't there?"

His droll observation made her smile, as it was intended to do. "Good or bad, isn't there always?"

"What was the beginning?"

"The night I met Mac."

"Then let's start there."

As simply as that, her story began. Once started, it poured from her. A fountain held in check too long. Words, cleansing words, that opened old wounds to the light.

She spoke of their days in college, of their different backgrounds. Of his reluctance and her determination. She didn't spare herself. The picture she painted of her immaturity was the unadorned truth, with no justification.

Lincoln, wise man that he was, only listened and did not judge. If he questioned how that selfish creature had become the woman he knew, it was answered when she spoke at last of Sarah. Sarah's short, tragic life. Her death. The effect she had on Jennifer's life.

"I could never deal with her death," Jennifer admitted. "Every year a few days before her birthday, a terrible melancholy that always seems to be with me becomes too much. I can't think. I can't function. So I drop out."

"And after a while, when you can function again, you drop back in." Lincoln made his first observation since she'd begun her story.

"Yes."

"Then you really haven't come close to accepting Sarah's death or dealing with it?"

"Never."

"Until now."

"I'm not sure I have yet."

"Wanting to is a beginning, Jennifer. Do you know why you want to?"

For the first time she couldn't meet his gaze. "I don't know."

"I think you do."

She was on her feet again. She could never be still when she faced a problem. The office was suddenly too close, too small. It took all her determination not to return to the window.

"Jennifer?" Lincoln prodded gently.

Biting her lips, she shook her head. "It's getting late."

"I have all evening."

"You've had a long day. You must be tired." Mac had said those very words to her what seemed like a lifetime ago.

"Part and parcel of working at Barclay." Lincoln dismissed her concern with his own version of her stock answer. "Now that we have that little delay out of the way, why don't you stop hedging and face the truth?"

"I'm not sure I know the truth."

"Then shall I tell you?" His voice was deep and soft and compassionate. "Shall I tell you that you finally want to deal with your own grief so that you can help Mac with his?"

Jennifer didn't bother to deny his assessment. She was too honest to deny the truth. "Can you tell me why, as well?"

"I can, Jennifer. But that one you have to face for yourself."

Another truth she couldn't deny. "So where do I go from here?"

"Considering this has been a dress rehearsal for what you've known you had to do all along, I'd say the next step is evident."

"Mac came to me when he was afraid he'd hurt me. He's hurting now, and I have to go to him. I have to tell him everything and pray that he understands and can forgive me."

"If he's half the man I think he is, he'll understand. And as for forgiving you, there's nothing to forgive."

"I'd like to think you're right."

"I am." Lincoln grinned. "Believe me, I am. I'm also something else."

His grin was the signal that this impromptu session was done. And she realized it truly was. He'd helped her to bring old feelings into the open. He'd been her sounding board, her dress rehearsal, as he called it. The rest was in her hands, and there was success in that. Once she'd been at the mercy of her own tragedy. Now she had hope.

A little afraid of what lay ahead, but on an upbeat note, she matched her mood to his, playing straight man to his gambit. "Oh, yeah? What else is that?"

"I'm hungry. How about dinner."

"So am I." For the first time in days, it was true. "Dinner would be wonderful. But not at A Cozy Little Place. I'm not quite ready for that yet."

Lincoln unfolded from his chair. When he reached the end of his great height, he extended a long arm and snatched his coat from a hook by his desk. "No problem. I know a joint down by the river where the hamburgers are ambrosia. For that matter, they make a great thing that looks like a fried flower, except it's an onion. Then there's a chocolate pie guaranteed to be like nothing mother ever made, and—"

"Enough! Enough! I'm convinced." Jennifer was laughing, as she hadn't laughed in a long while, as they left his office.

Jennifer picked her way through the tumult of cranes and heavy machines. In preparation for this venture, she'd worn slacks and sturdier shoes than she normally wore to work. As she hopped over a pothole, she was grateful for the foresight. Dust was heavy in the air, and the noise was deafening. A heavy tractor of some sort roared by. In the din and dust, a brawny arm scooped her up like a sack of grain and deposited her a yard away.

The hands that released her were gentle, and from a grimy face a pair of white teeth flashed a brilliant smile. "Hiya, Doc. Sorry about the ferrying job, but when you get too close to the tracks, the fallout can suffocate you."

She had to wait a minute to catch her breath. "Thanks, I think. You're Little Sam, aren't you? We met at A Cozy Little Place."

"Yes, ma'am." Sam pushed his hat back and Jennifer could swear a blush burned beneath his darkened skin. "I'm surprised you remembered."

"Considering that only Tiny is bigger than you, it would be hard to forget you." Indeed, when she'd stood between the two hale and hearty men, she'd felt like a sapling among redwoods. "Lucky for me you came along today when you did, or I'd be eating a mouthful of dirt."

"Anytime, Doc." The blush faded, but the grin remained. "What brings you here today?"

A second machine lumbered by. Conversation halted while the noise faded and the whirlwind settled. In that time,

Jennifer discovered she couldn't bring herself to ask Sam about Mac. "I, ah, came to see Tiny. Is he here?"

"Tiny? Sure, Doc. Tiny's always here. In fact I saw him go into the super's shack there by the gray truck."

"Thanks, Sam." She waved and would have walked away, but the big man caught her hand to detain her.

"Wait." From the seat of a smaller truck, he brought out a blue hard hat and, adjusting the straps, he fitted it on her head. Even at its smallest size, it promptly slid to her nose. Sam laughed and slid it back again. "Sorry it's not a better fit, but it'll have to do. Regulations."

"Right." She tapped the hat in a salute. Mac had teased her about a blue hat, promising her one of her own. She'd refused it, never anticipating she would be on the site, her head nearly swallowed by a hat meant for someone else. There were a lot of things she hadn't anticipated. Men like Sam and Tiny. That one day she would be searching for Mac. Her smile was a little wobbly. "Thanks, Sam."

"My pleasure, Doc."

The path to the super's shack was easier to negotiate. She was at the open doorway in less time than it took her hat to dislodge again. As she struggled to push it back, Tiny was there to meet her.

"'Mornin', Doc. I thought that was you."

"Good morning, Tiny." The hat slid with a thud to her nose.

"Having trouble?" The question was meant to tease, but a quick look at her face as she slid the hat back again sobered him instantly. Leading her into the shack, he took the hat and tossed it away. He didn't speak or question her until he seated her at a desk covered with charts and drawings. "Now, suppose you tell me what's wrong."

The chipper courage she'd shown Sam fled as Tiny patted her shoulder with a big paw. "I've been looking for Mac. I haven't seen him in days."

Tiny didn't speak until he'd drawn up a stool and sat beside her. Taking her hand, he looked down at her pale fingers. "Honey, he's gone. He has been all week."

"Gone? But he has a job to do here."

"No." Tiny shrugged his massive shoulders. "His part of the work has been over for some time. Mac was only here as a consultant. Some problems with the soil and the footings. He was free to leave weeks ago."

"But he stayed on."

"I think we both know why."

Jennifer wasn't sure she did. At the moment she wasn't sure of anything. "Did he say why he was leaving or where he was going?"

Tiny kept his eyes on their joined hands, and with his thumb he stroked the tips of her fingers. "He hadn't been himself for days. He was quiet and kept to himself. A few days ago he came in looking like the world had caved in on him. Said he was leaving, no excuses, no explanations. And just like that he was gone." He released her hand and straightened. "I can tell you, though, he was a man who was hurting."

"He didn't say *anything* to let you know where he was going?"

"Not a clue."

"Then I'm too late." She made no effort to hide her despair. "Too late for the second time in my life."

Helplessly, Tiny released her hand to pat her shoulder again. "Is there anything I can do?"

Jennifer stood and touched his cheek. "Thanks, Tiny, but there's nothing anyone can do now."

"I'll walk you back to the hospital."

"That isn't necessary. I can go alone." Her chin lifted and her eyes were dry but too bright as she retrieved her hat. "I'm accustomed to being alone."

Her small, brave figure had been swallowed by the flying dust before Tiny muttered an impotent curse and went back with half a heart to his work.

Rain was falling. Rain that began in the morning and settled in, turning the day gray and the night dreary. But Jennifer didn't care. All her days were gray now. All her nights dreary.

Pulling the collar of her coat closer and tugging the brim of her rain hat lower, she hurried across the parking lot. The hour was late. She was the only one who walked among cars that waited like great hulking shadows, her muffled step the only step that splashed through water gathering in a solid sheet over the pavement. Until a bulky shaped blocked her path.

"Working a little late, aren't you, Doc?"

She halted only inches from him, her face turned into the falling mist, looking into dark blue eyes. "Mac."

"We have to talk." His look bored into her, haunted, desperate.

"I know."

"About Sarah."

"Yes."

Without a word he took her arm. At her car, he opened the passenger door. When she was seated he went around to the driver's side and slid beneath the wheel. The windshield wipers made a sibilant sound as he drove through the rain.

Huddled in her seat, Jennifer ventured a question. "Where are you taking me?"

"To your home to pack a bag." He didn't look away from the road. "Then to mine."

It was on the tip of her tongue to refuse. To remind him she had a job and couldn't just leave. Instead, she kept quiet. It was spring. The census at the hospital was at a record low. No one was in crisis. One phone call, and her scant patient load would be in Lincoln's capable hands.

No one at the hospital really needed her. Only the brooding man who rode by her side. And as she settled back to watch the rain, Jennifer knew, though she would never have him, she needed him.

Ten

The rambling farmhouse was comfortable and unassuming, a charming, much-loved relic from the past. The kitchen was its soul, the great table, laden with food to break the night's fast, its heart. The family that gathered for the morning ritual, like the house, were earthy and warm.

They were Mac's family. And in a strange way Jennifer's family too.

To reach them Mac had driven into the night. Through Georgia and the Carolinas, each mile ticking off like clockwork, each wetter than the last. Rain had come down in torrents. Driving grew more and more difficult, requiring his complete concentration to steer the Cherokee through the blinding deluge. Jennifer sat quietly by his side.

She'd had no idea what he intended or even what he considered his home when he'd dropped her at her door, issuing a terse command to pack sturdy clothes. She hadn't questioned what he'd done while she prepared for the trip, nor how he managed the switch of her ancient Chevy for the Cherokee. She'd simply gone with him, sitting for hours in the closed quarters of the Jeep, only a word or a touch away, yet worlds apart.

Somewhere in the distance, in the gloom, in the flood, on a narrow winding road with no lights but their own in sight, she'd fallen asleep.

When she woke she was alone in a strange bed, surrounded by the first glow of sunrise, with the mouth-watering aroma of frying bacon a gentle summons. After one disoriented second she'd remembered the McLachlan farm, a fleeting impression of Dare and Jacinda, then, mercifully, a bed that smelled of fresh evergreen and promised rest.

Meeting the family again in the light of day was ridiculously effortless. Leaving the bed, she'd splashed water on her face and tugged a brush through her hair. Then she'd dressed in khakis and a shirt that had been thoughtfully taken from her luggage, and followed her nose. When she appeared at the kitchen door, Dare, an older version of Mac, looked up from the stove, grinned as if she was a permanent fixture at the farm, told her she was just in time and sat her at the table with a brimming plate before her.

From there the day went uphill as family members appeared, one by one, from morning chores. Jacinda, Tyler, Paul and Amy. And lastly, Ross, arriving from his own place, dressed in a lab coat and ready for a day at his office. Jennifer had met them all before at her wedding to Mac. Now she met them again. In ten years only the children had changed drastically. At seventeen, Tyler had grown into a quiet, dark-haired young man. The twins, eleven, boisterous and as alike as a boy and girl could be, were a far cry from the babies she remembered.

Only three were missing. Antonia, a reluctant star whose glamour and appeal survived marriage to Ross, finishing a rare film in Italy and anxious to be with her husband. Jamie, on tour, appearing on the concert stages of exotic and far-flung places.

And Mac.

His absence worried her, even as she smiled and laughed and puzzled over the family. No one seemed to think it odd that after ten years she and Mac were suddenly together. No one questioned. No one judged. She was simply Mac's wife, part of the family returned.

Would they be so charitable when they knew the truth? Or would they hate her for Sarah as much as Mac did?

"I think he's nuts." Ross set his plate by Jennifer's and took the chair next to hers.

Jennifer nearly choked, certain for an appalling instant the dashing physician had read her mind.

Paul piped up with "Nuts? Who?" saving her the need to answer.

"Your uncle Mac, of course."

"Oh." Paul shrugged, his mouth full of biscuit."You mean because he went off to do some dumb errand, instead of sleeping in with Jennifer."

"Paul!" Jacinda admonished with a quick apologetic glance at Jennifer.

"Out of the mouth of babes." Ross was chuckling as he spread jam over a biscuit of his own.

"Daddy said it first." Amy added her voice to her brother's. "I heard him tell Tyler."

"Oh, Lord!" Jacinda rolled her eyes. "These McLachlans, they're all alike." Then to Jennifer, "If you haven't seen that for yourself already, you will soon enough."

No, I won't, Jennifer thought, and the bright morning was tarnished.

"Tyler said Daddy was just jealous 'cause it was his morning to make breakfast and he couldn't sleep in with Mom."

"Amy!" This time Tyler did the scolding. "That's enough. We're making Jennifer blush." Tyler did not have McLachlan blood flowing in his veins, but his mannerisms were theirs. And like the McLachlans, his grin was devilish. "If you don't stop eavesdropping and then blabbing what you hear, little lady, your ears are going to grow to the size of saucers and your tongue as long as an eel."

"Yuck!" Amy threw her napkin at him.

"A long, slimy eel."

"Won't!"

"Will!" Not to be outdone, Paul took up the chant.

Grateful the attention had turned from her, Jennifer discovered she could smile at Jacinda's hand slipping into Dare's.

"Kids." Ross was laughing as he leaned closer to Jennifer. "Makes you glad you never had any, doesn't it?"

Jennifer lost her hold on her fork, and the blood ran from her face even as a hand closed over her shoulder.

"Listen to the man!" Mac's voice, Mac's hand. With it his strength. "He hates kids so much he made them his life's work."

"I know." Her voice was shaky, but no one seemed to notice. On a grateful impulse, she turned her head, touching her cheek to the back of his hand. The effect was electrifying, and she would have drawn away, but his hold on her shoulder wouldn't allow it.

The sudden blanching of her face hadn't escaped everyone. Ross's laughter fled, his dark eyes considered. His voice was pitched only for Jennifer. "Are you okay?"

Mac heard and answered for her. "She's fine." As he took the empty chair opposite Ross, he slid his fingers down her arm, to take her hand. As casually as if it was an ingrained habit, he lifted it to his lips. "Or she will be—" he breathed the words over her knuckles "—as as soon as I get her up to the lodge."

"No!" The clamor was instantaneous, and every voice joined in.

"Robbie!" He'd been Mac for a long while, but when Jacinda was disturbed, he was Robbie. "Do you really have to go so soon?"

"We really do." His lips still brushed over her knuckles. His gaze still held hers, but only Jennifer felt his hard grip. Only Jennifer saw the fire in his eyes. "We have a lot to talk about. A lot to explain."

"You can at least wait until after breakfast, can't you?" Jacinda turned her plea to Jennifer.

"I don't think so." Jennifer pulled her fingers from Mac's. Averting her eyes from that unfathomable stare, she folded her napkin by her plate. "Ten years makes for a lot of catching up, and I can't be away from the hospital long." She caught Ross's sudden look of surprise, but didn't address it. Mac's family didn't know what the giddy twenty-year-old they'd met only once had done with her life. But there were many things Mac's family didn't know. "We really have to make every minute count."

"All the supplies we'll need are in the Cherokee." Mac was standing now and his early-morning errand was explained. "As soon as you're ready, we'll be on our way."

Jennifer pushed back her chair. "If everyone will excuse me, I'm ready now."

Tyler was out of his seat, going with her to the stairs, offering to carry her luggage.

"Better get a jacket. We're heading into higher elevations and it could be colder," Mac called after her, and without waiting for a reaction, returned to his family.

"That was quite a performance."

The Jeep bumped over a rocky stream, through water rising to the hubcaps and up an embankment, before Mac answered. "I meant to be back before breakfast, I never intended for you to face them alone. For that, I apologize."

"They're good people, Mac. And now they think we're together again."

"I know."

Jennifer watched him, as light darting through the forest played over his features. "You planned it this way," she said half to herself. "You wanted them to assume..."

"Of course I did." He turned a stolid gaze to her. "Why else would I have Jacinda put you in my room? In my bed?"

"You slept there, too?"

"Of course. Did you think, Dare and Tyler, even Paul, were imagining things?"

"I suppose I thought they were mistaken."

"No mistake. You were very pretty with your hair tumbled across my arm." While she absorbed that bit of information, under his expert hand, the Jeep made an abrupt right turn and began a sharp climb.

The path they took was more rut than road. If it was traveled, it was only rarely. Mac battled the spinning, skidding Cherokee over rock and slippery shale before he spoke between clenched teeth. "Rest assured, my love—" sarcasm was sharp in the endearment "—that's all there was. You slept like a zombie and did nothing more seductive than curl against me."

"I'm sorry," she murmured, not certain it was the right response, but unable to think of another.

"Don't be. It isn't important. Not anymore."

They were climbing a wall of stone. Jennifer was certain it was perfectly perpendicular. Clutching her seat, she closed her eyes and kept them closed until the Jeep topped the incline. On an even keel again, she could almost think rationally. "I hate subterfuge."

"Do you now?" The irony was delivered without so much as a glance as he kept his attention on the trail.

"There's no pleasure in duping good people."

"There's no pleasure in causing unnecessary grief, either."

"You don't intend to tell them about Sarah? Ever?"

"I don't know." He looked at her then, long and hard. "I don't know anything anymore."

Then they were climbing again. The inclines were steeper, the rocks larger. Tensions thicker. Mac had neither time nor inclination for conversation, and Jennifer virtually reclined in her seat, questioning the sanity of coming to the end of the world, with a man who despised her.

"This it it. You can open your eyes now. We're home."

Home, Jennifer discovered when she finally opened her eyes, was the top of the world, not the end. Lodge was a misnomer for the sprawling structure of stone and glass and hand-hewn logs. The name implied rustic, even rough. But there was nothing either rustic or rough about Mac's lodge.

Jennifer gaped at its clean lines and uncluttered expanses, at the power and style that turned simplicity to magnificence. Leaving the car, she wandered an overgrown path to a stone wall. For as far as she could see there were mountaintops after mountaintops. The Blue Ridge, with smoky mists rising from hidden valleys. Turning again, she studied the building, as suited to the man as the landscape.

"You built this." Her gaze roamed from roof to beam and stone. "With your own hand, out of what you found here."

"With help from my brothers on occasion." He'd been only a step behind, waiting for her reaction. In spite of the fact that he tried not to care, he was pleased that she saw his stamp on the lodge. "And on other occasions a helicopter."

"Another little skill you picked up over the years?"

"When time was the important factor I couldn't always wait for a pilot."

"So you learned to fly yourself?" Jennifer said more to herself than to Mac.

"I learned to fly."

"In the jungle."

A noncommittal nod that left unsaid the danger, setting a cold hand about her heart. "In the jungle."

His real home for nearly a decade. Where he'd learned to do so many things, where he'd become the confident, capable man he was. Yet there was the lodge. He called it home. "Why did you build this?"

"It was something to do." He shrugged. "A place to come to when I was in the way. I liked the open spaces after the claustrophobic conditions of the jungle."

Jennifer understood claustrophobia. She understood it very well. "Why would you ever think you were in the way? Your brothers love you."

"Of course they do." He faced the mountain vista, his gaze fixed on some distant point. "But they have their lives. No one needs an intruder for weeks on end, no matter how loved he is. The lodge offered the excuse to give them the privacy they would've denied they needed."

"And when they helped, it was something you could share."

Mac leaned on the wall, plucked a stem of grass and chewed on it thoughtfully. Jennifer still surprised him with her insight. "You're pretty sharp, aren't you, Doc?"

Jennifer only shook her head. She wasn't so sharp. She hadn't drawn on some great wisdom to understand what the lodge represented. She understood, because she'd lived the same sort of life. A person apart, on the fringes, an observer, for whom free time to think was anathema. If Sarah had lived, if Mac had known her, perhaps she would have saved him. Perhaps she would have saved them both. Two people drifting in a world, with work their only anchor, the justification for existence.

But Sarah hadn't lived, and Mac had never known her. That was the bitter tragedy they'd come to resolve.

She shivered, and realized he'd been right about the temperature. The chill of winter still lingered in the highland. "If you'll show me to my room, I'd like to get settled before—" she paused and fought back a second shiver "—before we begin."

"Sure, Doc." He pushed away from the wall and flipped the stem of grass away between thumb and forefinger. "However you want it." He looked back as he led the way, taking in the colorless lips, the dark, sunken circles beneath her eyes. "The bed's all made, and I have some things to do. So there'll be time enough for you to sack out for a while."

Treading past one last tangle of dormant plants and a cluster of sweet-smelling hyacinths, he opened the door that was never locked. Moving aside without ceremony, he waited as Jennifer stepped into the place a lost man called home.

She didn't intend to sleep. In fact, she would have thought it impossible. But after exploring the bedroom that Mac designated as hers and after storing the little she'd packed in a handsome old cabinet, she sat down. Just for a minute, she told herself, a moment of respite from the strain, to savor the breathtaking view. But in the harmony of the room, with its high ceilings and soothing earthen tones, the fatigue that had become chronic dragged her down to peaceful oblivion.

"Mac?"

There was no answer. The house was quiet as Jennifer tiptoed from her room. At a front window she saw the yard had been tended. Weeds had been pulled away from the wall and the grass was shorter. A sling blade leaned against a stone, but there was no living creature in sight. She was alone.

Leaving the window, she went through the main part of the house. There were few rooms, but those few were large. Claustrophobia, a malady they shared. But a man who had spent his life in open spaces as he had would need huge rooms and twelve-foot ceilings. Indeed, with the ceilings, the skylights, singular beams where others would construct walls, and great expanses of window at every turn, Mac's house was as close as he could come to being outdoors.

One area, and that's what they were, areas, not rooms, flowed into another. A natural path of hardwood floors and scattered rugs, and she went with it. At the last turn, in what she judged was the back of the house, a fire blazed in a fieldstone fireplace. Wood was stacked in a bin by the hearth. A book lay facedown on a comfortably worn sofa, and a small table, before the ever present windows, was set.

In the adjoining kitchen a pot of spaghetti sauce bubbled and popped. A loaf of French bread was sliced, and slathered with butter. Lettuce drained in a colander in the sink. A bottle of wine had been uncorked.

The wine made her smile. Soave, a dry, white Italian. Not what the connoisseur would suggest to accompany spaghetti, but she'd never cared for reds. She understood, then, why Mac had been pleased when she remembered how he liked his tea.

While she'd slept, he'd worked. But Jennifer knew from experience that there are times when work was more restful than sleep. A change of pace for the body, narcosis for the mind.

There was nothing left to do in the kitchen, and she was drawn back to the fire. Hands shoved deeply in the pocket of her slacks, she looked up at a painting of two boys. No, she corrected, two very young men. Mac and Jamie at nineteen or twenty. Their hair was lighter then, their eyes more silver than navy. They weren't identical, but with their uncanny family resemblance, to the uninformed they would seem so. Perhaps the uninformed wouldn't notice that Jamie had a dimple or know that Mac was left-handed.

"Jacinda painted it." Mac stood barely inside the door, a cluster of daffodils in his hand. "Just before our lives took separate paths."

"You look so much alike. All of you," Jennifer murmured, her gaze on the flowers.

"Those who know our little ways, like Jacinda and Antonia, for instance, have decided that Ross and I are most alike, and Jamie could be a carbon copy of Dare. That particular duo made life interesting when we were growing up." At the sink, he filled a goblet with water and dropped in the flowers. Setting the scraggly bouquet in the center of the table, he suggested, "Dinner in ten minutes?"

"Sounds perfect." She was pleased that her voice was as low-pitched and composed as his, revealing none of her bewilderment at this new mood.

"There's a CD player by the books. Choose something you like. Thanks to a generator, we aren't completely without luxuries." With a wave of his hand he dismissed her to her choices, while he attended to the last of dinner.

Her thoughts in chaos, Jennifer thumbed through his selection of music. Mac was an angry man. A man who had every right to hate her. Yet he was acting like a friend or even a lover with seduction in his heart. It made no sense. Little in her life had since he'd come back into it.

Making a random choice, she slipped a disc she didn't bother to identify into the player and returned to the fire. The music began softly, simply, in sweet, mellow tones. A piano beneath a master's hands, and she knew it was Jamie. As she listened to the dreamy tune and watched the man she'd loved all her life, she wondered where the evening was going.

"One last bit of wine?"

"No!" She would have covered her glass with the palm of her hand, but she was a fraction too late. Mac had tipped the bottle over her glass even as he asked.

"It's your favorite with spaghetti."

With an apologetic sound, Jennifer pushed the glass away. She needed a clear head, and the little wine she'd already had was buzzing her brain. And they'd evaded what they had to face long enough.

"Why have you done this?" She gestured at the table, the food. The flowers. "You brought me here to settle something that's painful for both of us. In your mind I've done you a terrible injustice, and if I have you've every right to hate me. In that perspective this evening is madness."

"Perhaps there's method to my madness." He was watching her over the table. The sky behind him was fiery in sunset. The blaze in the fireplace danced in the fall of darkness. "And I have been a madman, make no mistake, since I learned I had a daughter."

Tossing down his napkin, he left the table. At the window he looked out at fire-rimmed mountains. "Tonight was to set a mood." He turned again to Jennifer. "I don't want to be angry, not when I hear about her. No matter what we were or are to each other, one thing will never change—you're the mother of my child. And for my child I want to be fair."

"Before you decide to continue hating me."

"I don't hate you, Jennifer." He shook his head. "I thought I did. I tried desperately to hate you. I nearly convinced myself that anyone who felt only revulsion for starving children 'with eyes too big for their faces and bodies too heavy for matchstick arms and legs' deserved hatred."

Hearing, verbatim, the rash words of a frightened girl, words that haunted her dreams, Jennifer bowed her head. In her heart she heard their echo still. Cruelty cried in her terror of losing him. That could never be called back. For which she had been punished in the cruelest way.

Mac regarded her tumbled hair, her half-hidden face. "For days I wallowed in grief. I wanted to hate you. I needed to hate you. Instead, I kept remembering calls I wouldn't take, letters I never opened. I saw the woman you had become. A woman I couldn't hate."

He drew a long, harsh breath and exhaled in a sigh. "I know there are things I don't understand, and there are things I need to know. The role your father played. Why you quarreled. Most of all I need to know about Sarah."

Jennifer lifted her head, her throat constricted. With a finger she touched the petal of a daffodil. "These were her favorites," she whispered. "She wanted to dance with daffodils beneath the sun, but her poor heart was too weak. So she danced with them in her mind."

"The drawing by the window in your kitchen is hers."

His thoughtful observation was not a question and needed no affirmation. Jennifer heard the strain in him, but she couldn't meet his look. "As young as she was she showed an amazing talent. Her random scribbles weren't always scribbles. Jacinda..." her voice broke. Catching back a sob, she continued, "The artist in Jacinda would've loved her."

"All my family would have loved her. They never had the chance." The biting comments tumbled out and immediately he was contrite. "But given my example and the fact you'd met them only once, you couldn't know that."

Jennifer said nothing. She couldn't refute the truth.

Mac backed away from the anger. He couldn't let it intrude, wouldn't let it touch his daughter. "Sarah was ill for a long time?"

"From her first breath."

Raking a hand through his hair, Mac turned to the sunset again. His thoughts were just as distant as they reached back in time. "You were alone."

Jennifer nodded, not realizing he couldn't see.

"Tell me," he said at last. Half turning, the firelight carving deep lines in his face, he murmured, "Tell me everything."

The fencing was done. Jennifer was as much relieved as apprehensive. After a time of composing her thoughts, she began the only place she could—with the day he left her.

"I didn't know I was pregnant when we quarreled. I didn't know for days. When you left I cried until I was ill. I suppose you could call it a grown-up tantrum." She wouldn't spare herself, not when only the truth would serve. "I was completely out of control. Nothing could console me. Finally my father insisted I see his physician. Thank God, he was a thorough, careful man who wouldn't prescribe medications until he knew his patients thoroughly. It was he who discovered I was pregnant. Just barely." Her voice, falling ever lower, sank now to a whisper. "Most likely from the last time we made love."

He stared woodenly into the fire. "So you called me."

"Yes."

"And you wrote."

"You know I did. Then I went to Rick's apartment and you were already gone."

"After that you never tried again?"

"No." Her answer scarcely rippled the air. "My father . . ." Even now she couldn't bear to think of what Edwin Burke had done. She couldn't deal with his betrayal. Of her. Of Mac. Of Sarah. "My father convinced me you wanted nothing to do with me or with the child."

Mac's arms were tight over his chest. His hands were fists. "You believed him?"

"There was no reason not to."

A bleak nod, dealing with the truth. He'd left and never looked back, making it easy to believe. "After Sarah was born you quarreled with him?"

"We quarreled long before then. He suggested an abortion. I refused. Then he demanded, and I refused. Ultimately he threatened to disown me."

"You refused again, and he carried out his threat." Mac had found a new channel for his hate. Edwin Burke and himself. "How did you live? How did you manage Sarah's care and your training?"

"I had jewelry and some stock. For the first time in her life, my mother went against my father. But only in secret. The little she gave me helped—it was enough to get me through the pregnancy. When Sarah was so ill, she helped more. There was a small legacy she'd never let him have control of. When he discovered she'd given it to me, he was livid. I try not to think of the hell he put her through."

"Bastard!" Mac's fists were clenching and unclenching, craving the useless but gratifying retribution of flesh pounding flesh.

"He was worse than that." Her voice was stronger for a moment, condemnation ringing in it. "After Sarah's death my mother's health deteriorated even more. I think she hadn't the heart to live any longer with a man who had become a monster. Before she died she'd discovered just how monstrous he'd been."

Mac knew what was coming. As certain as rage was rising cold and deadly in him, he knew. He wanted to hear it, for in it was salvation for Jennifer and himself. And yet for her, he hated the ugliness of it all. Standing, his body taut as a bowstring, he kept himself from going to her.

She had to face again what the man who had been the center of her young life had done to her. To them.

Her hands were twined now on the table, her fingers trembled with the force of her grip. She was a stark figure, neither bending, nor moving. "After you left for South America, I wanted to try one more time to reach you. My father stepped in again. He had contacts in the country and they could accomplish more than I. After a believable interval he told me he'd been right from the start. You wanted nothing to do with me ever again or with the child I claimed was yours."

"Claimed!" Mac's anger nearly choked him. He'd expected Burke's duplicity, but never this.

"He was my father. I trusted him. I stopped trying to reach you then."

"With that ammunition he put added pressure on you to have the abortion?"

"We argued long and bitterly. In the end, I was given a choice—my father or our child." She left the table to go to the fire. The flames licked at dried wood, ran the length of a log and burst into a hotter blaze. The heat enveloped her, but Jennifer felt she would never be truly warm. "I never saw him again. His choice. After Sarah died, when it was too late for all of us, when my mother discovered what he'd done, it was mine."

"Damn him!" Mac's hand made a solid thud against the window frame. "He cheated us! All of us! It's more than a child not having her father, or a father his daughter. He cheated us of our lives."

"If I'd been wiser—"

"No!" He'd crossed the room and was taking her in his arms as he spoke. Holding her against him, he was startled all over again at how small she was. More fragile than the last time he'd held her. Too fragile to deal with the trage-dies of her life alone. Yet she had. He and Edwin Burke had seen to that.

Cradling her cheek in his palm, he drew her head to his chest. "Don't think about him," he commanded in a soft, rough snarl. "Not ever again."

Marveling at the strength in her slim body, he held her closely, tightly. Until she nodded and bit by bit her body eased its rigid stance. Until she accepted his embrace and curled into him like a wounded child.

Gathering her up in his arms, he took her to the sofa. Holding her on his lap, stroking her hair as it spilled down her back, he listened to Jamie's music and stared into the fire, dreaming of what might have been.

He thought she slept, hoped she slept, but then she lifted her head and touched his cheek. "I should have known." Her face was ashen, her eyes dry and joyless. "Even if you didn't want me, you wouldn't desert your child. I should have known."

Clasping her hand in his, he brought her palm to his mouth. "No," he said simply, then lifted his head, his gaze returning to the mysteries of the fire. "He was your fa-ther." And in what was her perfect world, all little girls trusted their fathers. Then he spoke the most damning. "And I deserted you."

"Only because—"

"Shh." He brushed his lips against her hair. "Don't say anything. Just let me come to terms with it as it was. No qualifications. No excuses. The truth."

Jennifer subsided. She'd had her own guilt to come to terms with. Excuses had not made it easier to deal with. She wouldn't offer them to him now. Her arms slipped around his body. Her head rested against his shoulder. With her touch, she offered the only comfort he would accept.

The sun had disappeared, the fire burned low, and Jamie played on as Mac faced his demons and his loss.

Embers had turned to ash and the room had grown chilled when he sighed and stirred. When he rose, it was with Jen-nifer in his arms. When he took her to bed, it was his bed. When he took her in his arms, it was only to hold her.

Long into the sleepless night when he turned to her, tears on his face, she welcomed him. When they made love it was slow and tender, a bittersweet remembrance of time and love lost. When he caressed her she was, for that moment in the darkness, the wild, exuberant girl in a woman's body. The whimsical beauty who made his blood sing and his mind forget. When he kissed her he mourned for that bright, shining hoyden and for a young idealist, for sweet new passion and innocence. When his body joined with hers, he knew that for both of them it was the soothing of grief for their lost child, and much, much more.

She was sleeping at last when he rose from his bed to light the logs laid in a corner fireplace. He didn't know how long he'd been crouched there, lost in thought, when Jennifer touched his shoulder. When he looked up at her, she was naked, as he was naked, but so beautiful and fine it hurt to look at her.

"I didn't mean to wake you, Jennifer."

"I know." Her hair was hanging over one shoulder, touching the tips of her breasts as he wanted to touch her.

"You haven't slept enough in weeks."

"It doesn't matter, Mac. I have the rest of my life to sleep."

She was gazing down at him in the flickering light. The quiet desperation of their lovemaking was done, their wishful yearning reconciled, sorrow for a little while eased.

This was a new time, a new beginning, and he wondered what she saw, now, in him.

Nemesis? Friend? Lover?

"Our lives," he said, his gaze keeping hers. "What will they be after tonight?"

Again a shake of her head. Again the glorious fall of her hair brushing over her breast. "Perhaps Madame Zara could tell us our future, but I only know what I want for this night."

"What do you want, Jennifer? Tell me."

"This." Kneeling, she took his hands in hers, drawing him up with her. Stepping into his open arms, her own twined around his neck, her body teased his. Tugging his head to hers, even as she was rising on tiptoe, she breathed against his lips, "This. I want this."

The room was nearly silent. Only the sputter of the fire accompanied the sighs and whispers, the sultry, lazy laughter that followed half-caught gasps. Body skimmed over body. Arms tangled, legs twined. Mouths fused in deep, seeking kisses, then broke apart to follow the paths of wandering hands. Sinuous moves tantalized. Fevered responses intoxicated. Unspeakable pleasure as untamed as the land beyond the window, as breathtaking, left them trembling and hungering for more.

It was madness, wonderful madness that begat madness, and neither wanted to be sane again.

When she lifted her body over his, there were no bittersweet remembrances and no mourning for lost love. No yearning for sweet new passion, for innocence.

There was only this.

There was only now.

Jennifer was a woman, with a woman's strength, a woman's passions, a woman's needs. As she took him with her to the crescendo of that last shuddering ecstasy, he knew she was the woman who could hold him.

The woman he wanted for all time.

Eleven

"**D**o you like it?"

Jennifer turned her back on a field of daffodils to smile at him. "I love it. The flowers are beautiful. Sarah would have loved them."

Sarah would have...

The phrase came easily now. There were still tears. Sometimes Jennifer's. Sometimes Mac's. Sometimes both. But for nearly a week they'd wandered the mountain trails and talked. Of Sarah, of themselves. Each night they'd lain in each other's arms. Perhaps they would make love. Perhaps their day was too exhausting to do more than hold each other.

It was a time of struggle and healing for Mac. He was eager for every detail of Sarah's life. He had to know that her heart was too weak from birth, that there was never any chance for a transplant. He'd listened, eyes closed, head down, as Jennifer described how Sarah had gradually grown weaker until one morning she simply didn't wake up. He had to be assured that the small hospital in Mary Burke's hometown, and Jennifer's refuge, had been an extraordinarily fine facility. That everything had been done for Sarah that could be done. That she was comfortable and even happy to her last waking moment.

Jennifer hated the hurt for him, but he was compelled to hear it and feel it. He needed everything to cope with his loss and, no matter how she tried to ease it, his sense of having betrayed them. In telling him of their child, with her blond hair and Mac's deep blue eyes, she'd tried to dwell on the good things, the happy days. As she found how much good there was, how much happiness, Jennifer had begun to heal, as well.

Looking now at the bobbing field of daffodils, she knew that next year, on the day of Sarah's birth, the day of her death, she would mourn, as she would always mourn, then go on with her life.

"*I* love them," she added, thinking for once of herself, and took one more step toward healing.

"This was an old homestead." He led her to a clearing with an ancient, scraggly orchard at its edge. "The lady of the house must have loved flowers. They've gone wild over the years, but her love survives her in them." Catching her hand in his, he drew her to a stone, her back against his chest, his arms wrapped around her. "I was afraid they wouldn't be in full bloom before you left."

Before she left.

Jennifer hadn't wanted to think of leaving, but the time was near when she must. It wouldn't be fair to Lincoln or to her patients to be gone much longer. "I should go tomorrow or the next day. I need to look in on Jason and check on Chrissie Hanyon especially."

Mac only nodded. Perhaps he and Jennifer had lost a child, but because of that child, the medical field had gotten a gifted and dedicated member. There had been no one for Jennifer to turn to, no one to counsel either of them in that distant time and place. The specialty was small, but the need was great, and she had met it for others if not for herself. Once she'd rejected suffering children. Now she was their comfort.

She was never heartless, nor vengeful. He recognized that now, but there was more he had to know before his mind could be at peace. "Would you tell me something?"

"Anything." With his arms around her she could face anything.

"If I hadn't followed you to the cemetery, would you have told me about Sarah?"

Jennifer crossed her arms over his, her hands clasping his shirt. The sun was bright. Even at this altitude, the day was warm, but she was remembering another day. "I don't know. I honestly don't. At first I simply couldn't cope with telling you. When you came back, I'd already begun the morbid slide that always accompanies the anniversary of her death." Turning in his embrace, she framed his face with her hands. "But it wasn't completely selfish. A part of me wanted to spare you the agony and the loss."

"As I've protected my family."

"Then you believe I wasn't perpetuating the deception my father began?"

"I do now, but I was afraid that somewhere deep in your heart you felt I didn't deserve even this little knowledge of Sarah."

"Didn't deserve?" Her hands fell away from his face, her head turning from side to side in disbelief. "How could you think that?" she whispered. "Have you never realized why I kept your name? Hasn't it sunk in that I wanted my daughter to be your daughter? Don't you know yet that I loved you and all I had to give her was your name?" She gestured futilely, in frustration. "Oh, there were your pictures by her bed and stories of the great adventures that kept you from coming home, but your name was something real. Something nobody could take from her."

"Pictures? Stories? Does that mean she knew me and thought I wouldn't come home?" If he'd hurt before, it was nothing compared to this.

"No, love! No!" She grasped the lapels of his shirt as if she would shake him into believing. "It wasn't like that. You were her daddy and she loved you, but you couldn't come home. *Couldn't*, Mac. Never wouldn't."

He wasn't hearing her. "God, she must have hated me."

"Sarah never hated anyone. Especially not you." Aware that his arms had fallen to his sides, she stepped back. "I meant to keep this for another time, when you had better perspective. I can see now I should have. No matter what you believe, I gave Sarah a wonderful father. You were a part of her life, as special to her as the daffodils. She loved you."

He was listening now, a touch of awe in his look. "You created a fantasy, something she could to hold on to."

"None of it was fantasy. Every word I told her was true. Even that you couldn't come home." In a sigh she added what she'd never told Sarah. "Because my father and I drove you away." Her shoulders bowed, but only for a fleeting second. "You were right, Mac."

She'd said that before, and he hadn't understood and hadn't questioned her.

"No matter the outcome, you were right to go. I was wrong to stay." She backed away another step, shaking her head again. "I didn't mean to get into any of this. I've spoiled the day and this place for you."

"You haven't spoiled anything. You've been kinder than I deserve. I think I know why." He closed the distance between them. "I hope I know why."

"It doesn't matter now."

"You're wrong. It matters very much. You've never asked why, after one perfect night of lovemaking, I checked out of your life."

"What could I ask? I had no illusions that it was more than a night. I had no claim on you. We had no covenant, no commitment."

"Didn't we? I know what I said. No past? No future? All the talk and running in the world doesn't make that true. We do have a past. Our past is Sarah."

"And the future?"

"Why do you think I came back for you before I knew about Sarah and after? Of course I needed to hear about her, but it was more than that. I couldn't walk away as unfettered as I thought. I couldn't forget you. I didn't want to forget you. Then there was the chance you could be pregnant with my child again. A slim one, but a chance. God help me! I almost went crazy when I realized it. I'd lost you once, and our child, but I didn't intend to lose you again."

Jennifer's hand strayed unconsciously to her stomach. Her expression a mix of bewilderment and wonder. "You would want a baby?"

"Our baby."

"Even if I'd done the awful things you suspected?"

"I think I always knew you hadn't, but yes, even then."

"Why, Mac?" She was standing in his shadow, so close she could feel the heat of him, but not his touch.

"For the same reason you never believed I meant to hurt you. Why you kept my name and taught our daughter about me. Why you comforted me when you were hurting as badly. Why you made love with me, time and again, and called my name. Only mine, Jennifer, because there's been no one else."

One step brought their bodies into contact. Jennifer was afraid. More afraid than she'd been in a long, long time. "What are you saying?"

He touched her cheek, his fingers curving around it, his thumb stroking over her parted lips. "I'm saying I love you, Jennifer. I never stopped loving you. Just as you never stopped loving me."

She laid a hand on his chest to give herself space. "There's so much."

He didn't release her, didn't look away from her amber gaze. "So much between us. Some of it good, some of it bad, and we survived it all. It's taken us ten years, but now we have a second chance. I want that chance, Jennifer. I want a marriage and the children we might have. Most of all I want you."

"I'm not the girl you fell in love with."

"She's there." He smiled now. "She simply grew up and became the woman I don't think I can live without."

Her fingers curled into the fabric of his shirt, clinging, instead of holding him away. "Can it be?"

"Anything can be if you love me enough."

Tears spilled beneath the sweep of her lashes, but she made no move to wipe them away.

He couldn't lose her now. Not after all they'd survived. If he did, he would be doomed to spend his life as alone as he'd been the past ten years. The specter of another lifetime of loneliness made him desperate. And in desperation he gambled.

"I'm sorry." He touched a tear, his finger lingering at her cheek. "Perhaps I made a mistake." He backed away. "When you're ready I'll take you back to the lodge, and in the morning I'll drive you to Barclay."

Jennifer caught his wrist. "Please, not yet."

When he turned to her, her courage fled. But incredibly he was laughing, taking her back in his arms. Holding her as if he would never let her go. "Ah, sweetheart, I thought you'd never tell me."

"Tell you?" Her words were muffled against his chest.

"That you love me."

"But I didn't."

Putting her from him, his hand secure at her waist, he bent until their eyes were on the same level. "You did. You have in every way but the words. Is it frightening to say what we both know?"

She'd lived so long guarding her heart the words didn't come lightly. But she knew now that the heart she thought she'd guarded was his, and had always been his.

"Only a fool wouldn't love you, McLachlan." In a jerky move she scrubbed her tears away with the back of her hand. "And I'm not a fool."

Mac's delighted laughter boomed over the clearing. A less than gracious admission, but more precious because it hadn't come easily. He wanted to hold her close again, but there was something to be settled first. "Will you let me live with you and build a life with you?"

"You want to live with me?"

"Wherever your profession takes you."

Jennifer hadn't forgotten that once she'd refused him the same respect. "Why would you make that sacrifice?"

"It isn't a sacrifice. I love you, I know you need your work, and your patients need you. I wouldn't interfere with that."

"But your work! Your new business!"

"A consultant is his own business. It goes as he goes. I can and I will go anywhere with you."

"Anywhere?" She was smiling, a smile so radiant her tears were forgotten. "Even to the lodge where there's a fire burning with a rug in front of it, so right for making love on a long, lazy afternoon?"

"I think I like the way you say yes, sweetheart." Mac's exuberant shout echoed across the mountain a second before he swept her into his arms.

Sunlight streamed through skylights. Flames danced in the fireplace. A bottle of wine waited, warm and neglected, on the counter. A shirt flung haphazardly toward a chair lay in a heap on the floor, the last of a trail of clothing that led from the door to the rug before the fire.

Jamie's music drifted around two lovers. Bits of distracted conversation blended with the melodies.

"We'll need a new ring to replace the one you hocked."

"Sold, McLachlan. Sold."

"For Sarah."

"Only for Sarah."

For a time there was silence and music and laughter. Delighted, triumphant laughter.

"We have to tell Dare and Jacinda."

"Ross and Antonia."

"Tiny and Sally."

"Madame Zara."

"Lincoln."

"The world."

"And Jamie."

"Who has a dimple here, while yours is—"

"Don't even think it, unless you want trouble."

"I like trouble."

"You asked for it, Doc."

"I did, didn't I?"

Silence. Music. Then words he'd waited to hear again.

"I love you, McLachlan."

And words she could never hear enough.

"I love you—" music played, the fire burned, then softly, ever so softly "—McLachlan."

*   *   *   *   *

Take 4 bestselling love stories FREE

Plus get a FREE surprise gift!

Special Limited-time Offer

Mail to Silhouette Reader Service™

3010 Walden Avenue
P.O. Box 1867
Buffalo, N.Y. 14269-1867

YES! Please send me 4 free Silhouette Desire® novels and my free surprise gift. Then send me 6 brand-new novels every month, which I will receive months before they appear in bookstores. Bill me at the low price of $2.24 each plus 25¢ delivery and applicable sales tax, if any.* That's the complete price and—compared to the cover prices of $2.99 each—quite a bargain! I understand that accepting the books and gift places me under no obligation ever to buy any books. I can always return a shipment and cancel at any time. Even if I never buy another book from Silhouette, the 4 free books and the surprise gift are mine to keep forever.

225 BPA AJH6

Name	(PLEASE PRINT)	
Address	Apt. No.	
City	State	Zip

This offer is limited to one order per household and not valid to present Silhouette Desire® subscribers. *Terms and prices are subject to change without notice. Sales tax applicable in N.Y.

UDES-93R   ©1990 Harlequin Enterprises Limited

He staked his claim…

HONOR BOUND

by
New York Times
Bestselling Author

previously published under the pseudonym Erin St. Claire

As Aislinn Andrews opened her mouth to scream, a hard hand clamped over her face and she found herself face-to-face with Lucas Greywolf, a lean, lethal-looking Navajo and escaped convict who swore he wouldn't hurt her— *if* she helped him.

Look for HONOR BOUND at your favorite retail outlet this January.

Only from…

Silhouette

where passion lives.   SBHB

Share in the joys of finding happiness and exchanging the
ultimate gift—love—in full-length classic holiday
treasures by two bestselling authors

JOAN HOHL
EMILIE RICHARDS

Available in December at
your favorite retail outlet.

Only from ▼ *Silhouette* ® where passion lives.

SILHOUETTE.... Where Passion Lives

Don't miss these Silhouette favorites by some of our most popular authors!
And now, you can receive a discount by ordering two or more titles!

Silhouette Desire®

#05751	THE MAN WITH THE MIDNIGHT EYES BJ James	$2.89	❏
#05763	THE COWBOY Cait London	$2.89	❏
#05774	TENNESSEE WALTZ Jackie Merritt	$2.89	❏
#05779	THE RANCHER AND THE RUNAWAY BRIDE Joan Johnston	$2.89	❏

Silhouette Intimate Moments®

#07417	WOLF AND THE ANGEL Kathleen Creighton	$3.29	❏
#07480	DIAMOND WILLOW Kathleen Eagle	$3.39	❏
#07486	MEMORIES OF LAURA Marilyn Pappano	$3.39	❏
#07493	QUINN EISLEY'S WAR Patricia Gardner Evans	$3.39	❏

Silhouette Shadows®

#27003	STRANGER IN THE MIST Lee Karr	$3.50	❏
#27007	FLASHBACK Terri Herrington	$3.50	❏
#27009	BREAK THE NIGHT Anne Stuart	$3.50	❏
#27012	DARK ENCHANTMENT Jane Toombs	$3.50	❏

Silhouette Special Edition®

#09754	THERE AND NOW Linda Lael Miller	$3.39	❏
#09770	FATHER: UNKNOWN Andrea Edwards	$3.39	❏
#09791	THE CAT THAT LIVED ON PARK AVENUE Tracy Sinclair	$3.39	❏
#09811	HE'S THE RICH BOY Lisa Jackson	$3.39	❏

Silhouette Romance®

#08893	LETTERS FROM HOME Toni Collins	$2.69	❏
#08915	NEW YEAR'S BABY Stella Bagwell	$2.69	❏
#08927	THE PURSUIT OF HAPPINESS Anne Peters	$2.69	❏
#08952	INSTANT FATHER Lucy Gordon	$2.75	❏

AMOUNT	$	
DEDUCT: **10% DISCOUNT FOR 2+ BOOKS**	$	
POSTAGE & HANDLING	$	
($1.00 for one book, 50¢ for each additional)		
APPLICABLE TAXES*	$	
TOTAL PAYABLE	$	
(check or money order—please do not send cash)		

To order, complete this form and send it, along with a check or money order for the total above, payable to Silhouette Books, to: *In the U.S.*: 3010 Walden Avenue, P.O. Box 9077, Buffalo, NY 14269-9077; *In Canada*: P.O. Box 636, Fort Erie, Ontario, L2A 5X3.

Name: _____

Address: _____ City: _____

State/Prov.: _____ Zip/Postal Code: _____

*New York residents remit applicable sales taxes.
Canadian residents remit applicable GST and provincial taxes.

Silhouette